September Love

Christine A. Adams

<u>Copyright</u>

Chapter One

It was an improbable, impossible week at work. As Manager at Morgan Stanley, one of the largest investment firms in Boston, actually in the country, Derek Holland had just lived through the September 15, 2008 Wall Street disaster. They called it the beginning of a recession but later when they heard that Lehman Brothers was failing, the insiders in the business knew it was much more than that.

The very next day, Derek knew he had to get away to clear his mind. So he packed his RV and headed north for some "off season" camping at Sebago Lake. Intuitively, he understood this trip was more a matter of survival than impulse.

As he drove up the Maine Turnpike, he began to relive the eighteen months since the accident outside of Boston where he lost he lost his wife, Jenny, and son, Zack. It was an unusual accident, the collision of two commuter trains.

The conductor, Phil Edmundton, died when the two-car train he was operating struck the back of another train as he was approaching Woodland Station outbound on the green line at about 6 PM. Somehow he missed the signal. Unfortunately, he took others to their death with him. Jenny Holland, a young mother, and Zack Holland, her seven year old son were two causalities.

As Derek's mind drifted back to that time, stark images of black twisted steel surfaced. The scene with blue uniformed helpers, struggling emergency workers in bright orange, and a sense of urgency and horror. Then he saw the dead faces of Jenny and Zack appearing slowly until they took over his whole mind and refused to dissipate into memory. They were still images etched in grey and black with diffused borders that entered stealthily, slowly descending like ghosts into his mind's eye. He recognized the form of Jenny's face and the sweetness of Zack's mouth and eyes.

An agitated motorist beeped his horn warning him as he drifted into the wrong lane. Derek shook his head once as if to shake the image out of his mind, and, then again, to bring him back to the reality of the moment.

I didn't think it could get any worse Derek thought as he sped along. Jenny and Zack gone. He felt the tears begin to well up in his throat. Now this. A tinge of fear gripped him. It was always that tightening in his stomach that got his attention. I could lose my job too. Hell, everyone could lose their job. Automatically, the investor in him began to assess the finances. What would be left? What could he sell? Where could he live?

Suddenly, he started to smile to himself thinking that nothing could compare to the loss he had just lived through. Even homelessness couldn't compare to the loss he already felt. Suddenly, he realized he'd been prepared for this threat of loss. The accident was a life changer for me-not some disaster, some tragic error, or whatever it was that Channel 5 kept saying. He knew he had found the only good anyone could ever say about losing his wife and child. Now, he could face any serious loss and live through it.

When Derek was a young man, he'd been a camp counselor at Camp Sunshine in the Sebago Lake area. Fondly, he remembered the lazy days swimming in the lake, teaching the boys how to fish. Because the boys were terminally ill, the counselors did more than teach swimming and fishing. They taught the boys to "live on." He remembered the peace sitting alone by the fire after the boys went to bed. Now, he longed for any peace! Instinctively, he recognized his need to return to the lake. Now, Derek needed to find a way to "live on."

Stopping at the rest stop on 95, he ordered a large coffee at the Burger King. The fatigue was beginning to set in. Every bone in his body felt heavy. He had lived on caffeine these past few months. Making his way up the Pike past Portland, he willed himself to stay awake.

God, he remembered those long days at the office right after the funeral. Twelve hours a day! Never stopping to feel or think. Just working every minute. Now I don't know how I made it. Work, and more work, I guess. The worst thing was going home. Couldn't do it some nights so I slept downtown, or at work. Now my work could be gone too.

Derek felt dazed by the decline in the market, the puncturing of the subprime mortgage bubble. It was a series of moments of "What's next?" But I have to keep going he thought as he automatically checked the rear view mirror to see if his small car was still hitched behind him. He adjusted the mirror, took another sip of the hot coffee and slowed down when he saw the Maine State Police up ahead.

Grateful to have anything to think about, anything to attend to, he kept his mind on the road. Carefully, he listened to the persistent voice bursting from the GPS. In 4.5 miles take a right onto Highway 261. He tried not to think. But then as he made his way over to Sebago Lake, the country roads were more familiar, more relaxed. Inadvertently, he replayed the day of the accident in his mind much as he did every time there was time for thought.

At work, Derek was interrupted by a late afternoon call. Someone was disturbing his hurried work as he tried to record the transactions of the day in a client's folder. He promised to meet Jenny and Zack at the Red Sox game.

Baseball was Zack's thing. The Red Sox his team. He was seven and played Little League ball with the Hingham Pirates. His uniform was not the conventional red or blue stripe but black and white, a perfect match for his black curly hair. Derek was nervous when his son went to bat because the boy took every swing personally. His dream-to hit like "Papi" of the Boston Red Sox.

"Mr. Holland," the official voice on the phone said bringing Derek back to the moment.

"Yes," he said as he straightened in his chair.

"We don't want to alarm you but there's been an accident. The T heading to Boston - a serious accident-two trains collided."

Derek put his hand to his head and gasped.

"Your wife and son are being treated at the Mass General. Can you come right away?"

"Are they alright? he cried out, now standing and shaking all over.

"We're doing the best we can," the tired voice said.

"Yes, yes thank you."

Leaving his papers on the desk, Derek grabbed his coat and sprinted to the parking lot below. In a frenzy, he made his way to Fruit Street pulling into the parking lot without taking a ticket. Running through the front lobby to the emergency room, he was greeted by the awful sight of nurses hustling between gurneys with broken bodies.

"Jenny Holland! Zack Holland!" He shouted to anyone who would listen. Someone directed him to a curtained cubicle. The traumatic sights and sounds of that night became imbedded in his brain as he ended that day, not at a Red Sox game, but identifying the bodies of his wife and child. These sights and sounds became a permanent memory in his psyche-and he ran from them every day and especially every night.

At first, it didn't seem real to Derek. Every night when he was on the subway, he would think he was just ending the day going home to Hingham. To the comfort of his white colonial two-story house with its sculptured lawn and shrubs on 113 Elm St. Then, he realized that the comfort was gone. Then, the memory flashed into his mind. The constant media barrage of coverage of the accident added more visuals to the permanent visual slide show in his mind. The scene of the train wreck, the testimony of those who survived. He knew he shouldn't watch but he couldn't pull himself away.

Automatically, it was Channel 5 Boston, or 10 New England, that he turned to. Inevitably, his wife and child's image would appear-along with every gruesome detail that became his own. Somehow he thought if he saw Jenny and Zack again, they might come back. This might be a nightmare!

In the early weeks, Derek stumbled through the memorial and burial with the help of his own family, and, of course, Jenny's Mom and Dad. Somehow, he deferred decisions to her parents who were as broken as he was. They all just moved by rote. It wasn't as if Derek had no feelings, every night he cried, heart wrenching sobs that wracked his body. Every time, he saw his son, Zack's, face, this beautiful dark haired boy with lively innocent eyes, he wept again. Sometimes he starred at Jenny's picture for hours, or replayed their videos thinking he might keep her memory alive.

Then in a few months, when the media cycle changed and he finally put his pictures in a special place, except his favorites which he kept beside his bed, he stopped crying every night.

It was at this point that he realized the subprime mortgage crisis was becoming a crisis at Morgan Stanley. There were meetings and more meetings. Contact with clients, trying to reassure them and contact with his brokers to also reassure them. As the situation at work became more desperate, Derek willingly drowned himself in his work. Now to save his company, the only thing left.

But as the months went on, he began to lose hope, and burn out physically with weight loss and fatigue. This was his condition on September 15, 2008, the day of the Wall Street disaster, with Lehman Brothers about to fail and Morgan Stanley in trouble. Completely exhausted he approached the entrance gate at Sebago Lake.

No reservations needed. Just drive up to the gate, write down the dates, pick a site, and put a check in the brown box. No one had to know where he was for a few days. He would call his boss when he could but he knew there was little he could do for now.

Derek picked site #148 because of its unencumbered view of the lake. As he began to set up, he barely noticed a small tent tucked into the corner of #149 or the figure lying on the beach beside a beach chair. He unhitched his Mazda Miata from the back of his RV and backed into the extra space on the site.

Of course, he was destined to remember other times when the family pulled into Sebago. The image of Jenny's slight figure came back. Her dark silken hair cut in a straight "bob" that framed her face and moved when she turned her head. Watching her move was like listening to a perfectly played Chopin Nocturne. She was light and smooth yet filled with ripples of sound that were both soothing and exciting.

Jenny would direct him into the campsite with little gestures to come forward, or move left or right. Zack would climb up on the front seat delighting in being with Daddy "upfront".

"Ok, Daddy, go back now. Stop!"

When the Flair was in its spot, Jenny always said "Good job", whether it was crooked or not.

"Good job, Daddy," echoed Zack.

"Good job, Buddy," the father repeated. The little boy's eyes always sparkled in the light of his father's approval.

On these trips, Derek was always teaching the little boy, "You put this bar down now and lift this lever." The boy watched and listened.

"Now we get the hose and plug it in."

"Over here, over here," the father pointed to the faucet. "And now we plug in this cord so we will have electricity. We need that!"

"We need that," the child said mimicking the same tone as his father, following a few steps behind him.

"Sweetheart, do you know where the red and white checkered tablecloth is?" Jenny would call out.

"Look in the box under the front seat." Derek was great at remembering where everything was so Jenny often relied on his memory.

"OK, got it! We're good!   I'll make some sandwiches," she would say as she opened the frig in the RV. Yeah, he thought, things with Jenny and Zach were always good.

Then, Derek realized that this was the first time he'd taken out the RV since they were gone. A wave of nausea swept over him.   Too many memories-too painful-he thought. A shiver of fear went through him. Several times last summer he thought of camping and even made a trip over to Overland's RV place to see if he could sell it. When he found out the RV had depreciated so much, he decided to keep it. Now, once again he wasn't sure.

After Derek fixed himself a snack, the nausea and fear left and fatigue overcame him so he decided to lie down for a few minutes. He drew the curtains in the bedroom area to darken the room and as he dozed off, he could hear the rhythm of the waves on the shore. Exhausted, he slept dreamless through the rest of that day and night until 6AM the next morning.

Derek didn't know that he was not alone in his need to escape. Earlier that week Ingrid Mikkleson, on her yearly pilgrimage to Sebago Lake, had found her way to the little tent on site #149, to become the slight figure sleeping on the far side of the beach. The one he barely noticed.

Chapter Two

Ingrid looked down at the odometer as she sped along Route 95 on her way to the Sebago Lake Region. Mindlessly, she paid the toll after greeting the toll taker as if this woman was one of Svein's parishioners, "And how are you today? Thank you <u>so</u> much." She automatically smiled into the tired, complacent face of the toll lady who seemed grateful to have any pleasant conversation headed her way. However, the toll taker did not return the smile.

Ingrid realized that it had been two years since she had to greet any parishioners at Grace Lutheran. Had it really been two years? How could that be? Two years? Sometimes it feels like a week, or two months, and sometimes it feels like forever. I guess I'm better than I was. They say there's a definite progression to getting out of grief. Elizabeth Kubler Ross' progression. Like shock, denial, and all that.

Sometimes when you're going through it, it's hard to remember those stages she thought. Yes, stages. That's it!

It can't be that definite for everyone. You miss a husband you loved- more than a husband you didn't even like. I know some women from Grace Lutheran that would be glad to be rid of a husband. Their stages could never be the same as mine. Just not as deep. More superficial, I guess.

"You're in shock," Carla said to me in that first week. I guess she was right but it didn't seem like shock. It was more like walking in a trance, doing everything by rote. I had to push my body to do what my mind told it to do. And it did it. Like getting dressed in a simple black dress for the funeral. Buying Kari an appropriate black suit with a ruffled collar, and the black shoes. Sneakers wouldn't do at a funeral memorial service for the daughter of the Senior Pastor.

And when things went wrong, when things got out of order like when the flowers got delivered to the wrong funeral home, I didn't get upset. I cried because it seemed too heavy a mistake to try to fix. When Annie, Svein's secretary fixed it with a simple phone call, I could see that it was just a little detail. I felt a little foolish crying so hard over that but it was OK. Everyone was solicitous because I wasn't supposed to react normally. After all, who finds their husband dead in his chair in the parsonage?

Shock might be fixating on a small thing like the scarf to wear to the funeral. What color? One with too much color might not be appropriate but the dress needed some color. Wouldn't people understand that the dress needed color. Probably not!

Seeing the scarf lying on my bed, Svein's and my bed, Kari had said, "Mom are you going to wear this scarf with your dress?" I didn't know how to answer her so I simply put on the scarf with black, blue, magenta and purple accents. I just let her question make the decision for me.

But it wasn't the scarf that stuck in her mind these last two years. It was the look of death on Svein's face that day when she found him. He was slumped down in his oversized black leather chair. Her thoughts kept returning to that look, that blank white stare that was unmistakably death. It came like a single frame in a movie. Suddenly, there on the screen of her mind. Sometimes in her dreams it reappeared. Every time it jolted her. Maybe that's what they mean when they say "shock"?

How is it that one moment can implant itself in your mind she thought. One sight that gets stuck and won't let time erase it. Every other moment moves on but that moment recreates itself. Maybe I'm bringing it on myself. I'm not moving through the stages of grief the way I should. Maybe I'm just crazy, she thought.

There were grief therapy sessions at the church for those who are "experiencing" grief. Ingrid knew she should go, so she did. Self conscious, unwilling to believe she had to. The corridor to the room behind the vestibule seemed longer on those nights. Her reluctance to go was evident in her slow stride, and in the fact that she always arrived late. But once in the room, she spoke of Svein to people who knew him and loved him. She left feeling better.

It may be stupid to come all the way north just to think, and re-read my journals. But what's stupid? She learned in grief therapy that nothing is stupid if it makes you feel better. I always get something out of this trip. This will be my third time visiting Sebago in September. Maybe I'll give it up someday. For now, I need to do this. It feels right to come to a peaceful place-no rules, no bells ringing to get me to my next class. Just the lake and peace. It's only September 13th and we don't start school until the 25th. I have the time now.

She increased her speed as she passed the Portland Mall on her left.

When she pulled into Sebago State Park, no one was at the gate. Not unusual this time of year she thought. Now let me see. There are envelopes here and a slot. Quickly, she made out a check for the proper amount and checked off the days. If I wanted to stay longer I could. She remembered the routine from last year. It comforted her. Anything that was routine seemed to comfort her.

"I hope number 149 is open," she said to herself as she slowly drove down the narrow dirt road to the lake shore. It was her favorite site right on the water. Off season was perfect on 149 but in season it might be a problem, right across from the kid's playground.

"It's open." She smiled and waved at the park attendant, an old man in his seventies, making rounds in a golf cart. Then she quickly claimed the most desirable site as her own by driving her PT Cruiser right in. It was "first come, first serve" in September and she was "first come" to 149. When she stepped out of her car, she stretched her arms over her head reaching for the sky. The sun warmed her as she began to pull the camping gear from the trunk.

"Nice day," the park attendant said as he circled by.

"Very Nice," she offered.

"Hope we don't get rain," he replied absently as he remembered her from previous years. A pretty woman to be out here camping alone but she's no trouble he thought. Ingrid smiled and nodded as she pulled more camping gear out of the trunk.

Neighboring campers looked on with curiosity. Why is it people seem distrustful of a woman camping alone? A bit annoyed, she wondered what harm could she do to the family in the Pop-Up on # 147, or to the retirees in the RV on # 146. Oh well! The kids will have to go back to school tomorrow and the older folk will find the nights too cold for a fire and leave.

"Never mind," she whispered to herself knowing that soon she'd be all alone enjoying "off season" at Sebago. Methodically she laid out her tent, drove in the stakes with a sure hand and raised the simple canvas frame with confidence. Her own slight frame was solid and fit from her daily runs and Yoga. Although in her forties, she moved with the grace of a woman in her twenties.

When the other campers lost interest in her, she dragged her chair down to the beach. Immediately, she felt a surge of relief as the brilliant gray blue water greeted her-sparkling and dancing like it often does in the Maine September sun. The soothing sun warmed her. The lake lapped the shoreline like a child licks an ice cream cone. The rhythm became a comforting song. The longing inside began to dissipate. In the quiet, she remembered her daughter, Kari. How proud Svein would be seeing her go off to college this morning. How she wished he could've been there with them. Silently, she absorbed her surroundings and relived her morning with Kari.

As they drove towards Storrs they were both quite anxious to see the campus again. "There's the sign-the University of Connecticut," Kari said a bit excited and a bit apprehensive.

"I see it," her mother answered trying to see out the back window of her fully loaded PT Cruiser. The car looked like a stuffed jewelry box with shades of pink and purple showing in the square windows. There was a pink and purple comforter, a small purple hassock, a coffee pot, pink sheets and blanket crammed into the back seat with all of Kari's clothes. They laughed all the way realizing how stupid they looked.

As they drove onto the Storrs campus, they noticed the unusual activity. Seemed like the whole freshman class was arriving at the same time-all carrying their things into the freshman dorm. Kari and Ingrid joined them. Still laughing and enjoying the day.

Sometimes it was difficult to distinguish mother and daughter as they carried in their pink and purple treasures. Kari, just 18, who had the same blond hair as her mother, was a bit slimmer and wore very tight jeans, with a shirt that was more revealing than anything her mother ever wore. From a distance Ingrid looked more like her older sister with the same blond hair and navy pants accented by a classic white sweater.

Finally when they finished setting up the room, Ingrid, not wanting the day to end said, "Let's go to the Co-op for lunch." Kari was famished so they walked past the Student Union building, the athletic complex where the UConn Huskies played basketball, and, of course, right by the Junior and Senior dorms.

Inside the Co-op, Kari steered her mother to the counter where they ordered a soup and salad lunch. The napkins and silverware were conveniently stacked on the cart by the window. Even though this was Freshman Move-In day, it was early so the cafe was unusually quiet. Settling at the table by the window, the daughter turned the conversation to Ingrid.

"Are you okay?"

"Fine, sweetheart, just fine."

Kari noticed a tired look in her mother's eyes. She worried about her. There was always a steady persistent worry in the back of her mind. She noticed that under all her pink and purple stuff, her mother packed her tent, tent heater, Coleman lamp and the small cooler. It wasn't that her mother didn't know how to camp; it was that she was doing it alone. Kari knew her mom was waiting for the results of a biopsy and hated to think of her alone in the Maine woods at this time.

"Are you sure you feel like driving all the way to Sebago today?"

"I'm half way there-besides, it gives me time to think, to get out of myself, you know -" her voice trailed off.

"When do you get the test results?" Kari asked trying not to sound anxious but failing.

"Dr. Bacon said about a week. I'll call him on my cell."

Kari looked down. "Call me, right away."

"Of course. It's fine dear. I just need time to be alone- to write in my journal." Ingrid said reassuringly as she reached out to touch her daughter's hand. Finally, Kari looked up.

Then a wry smile crept across the mother's face, "To start missing you!" They both laughed. After they ate lunch, Kari got up and suddenly hugged her mom.

"I'm just worried. I don't know what I'd do if I lost you too."

"I know, I know. Just remember how we did it the last time I had a biopsy. And after your Dad died-we went day by day and didn't worry until we had something to worry about."

"But the last time it was benign," she hesitated, "I just didn't expect to have it happen again."

"Dr. Bacon says it does sometimes," the mother reminded her daughter. Then more sternly, "You need to get settled and start your college life. No more worry!" Kari sat back absorbing her mother's reassuring words. Her expression softened.

Later, saying goodbye was tearful for both of them.

Now alone on the beach, Ingrid looked out at the island offshore with its green pines, spiky and straight, standing tall as soldiers. She gathered strength from them feeling a kinship to the area. Remembering the hard grey rocks that dotted the shoreline, and the soft caramel colored sand that sinks when you step into it. A cool September breeze cut across her shoulders.

Sometimes her thoughts were punctuated with the distant cry of the loon. It always touched her every time; it startled her because she felt that cry inside. When she looked back over the lake, an afternoon breeze was redistributing the ribbons of dark blue, cutting them, shifting them bringing change closer to her. A large bald eagle was soaring in the benign clouds, waving its wings to her.

Suddenly, she felt the same emotion welling up within her as that moment when she left Kari at UConn that morning. I can't hold her back she thought. She needs to make her own way. We've been trying to protect each other too much. It's just not healthy.

It's funny how you can know something but never speak of it. Sometimes we're like that with each other. A silent contract of some kind, I guess. Part of grieving had been making changes, like moving to the condo in Glastonbury. I just knew it was right. So different from the parsonage but so right.

In her mind's eye she pictured the improbable pink rugs and the delicate feminine aura of the place. She remembered the feeling she had when she first saw it and the reaction Kari had as well. An oasis for them from the parsonage years. So refreshing!

Not that the parsonage years were so bad but in some ways they were oppressive. The life of the Sunday Sermon, and Thursday night Women's Guild Spaghetti Suppers. A collage of events came barreling across her mind-weddings, funerals, and baptisms.

She shivered as she remembered the relentlessness of the church duties. "Service" they called it, or "his calling". But there were many nights she and Kari waited home alone, waiting for Svein to finally come home. They learned early on to be there for each other, to rely on each other. Their loneliness was part of his "calling to service."

"The girls," she said aloud. He always called us his girls. Just a sign of affection not a sexist remark. After a few minutes, the sun would blast out and drive her into the water. The coolness enveloped her body as she dove in. It was biting and softly sensual at the same time.

She smiled remembering the warmth of Svein's body when she woke up in the middle of the night. How she loved that warmth. She and Kari endured his busy schedule knowing there would be special week-ends in the cabin at Sebago Lake. It was a small cabin owned by the Grace Lutheran congregation since the 1930's. Anytime they could make a sweet escape from the prying eyes of the congregation, they did.

Now she was here again. A perfect day. Ingrid watched as an older couple pulled their travel trailer into a site down by the bathrooms. The old man raised his voice when his wife couldn't direct him into the spot.

"I can't see you, Eleanor."

"I'm right here," she said waving her arms around in some indistinguishable pattern known only to them. Eventually, they got the big rig into the area. Then, they did the usual older couple camping things. They fixed the picnic table for supper, set out chairs by the fire pit, put down the awning, talked to each other about trivial things; and finally, she settled down to read the newspaper. Eventually, he got out his fishing gear and trudged off through the woods to his special spot out on the rocks. Then, she went inside to take a nap. Ingrid envied their seemingly comfortable, yet mundane, existence together.

Another cool September breeze cut across her shoulders.

"I'm glad I came," she thought as the afternoon sun began to dim. Reluctantly, she left the beach moving her chair back to #149. In the time she was down by the lake, her neighbors on site #`147 and # 146 had packed up leaving the silent beauty just for her. The welcome silence punctuated the sad spaces still there in her heart and let them spread out over her body. She sighed with relief knowing she would finally be alone with her thoughts and feelings.

In her small tent was a comfortable bed, a Coleman heater and lamp to read by. On a folding table were her books and journal. Each day since Svein died, Ingrid kept a daily journal. This time of silence allowed her to re-read her journals as she sat by the fire. She burned each page after reading. It was her ritual-her way of honoring the past and accepting the future.

Before the darkness of the night settled in, she lit the Coleman lamp, built the fire and made herself a sandwich from her cooler. The fresh air made her hungry, so the simple bread, ham and cheese tasted especially delicious. Eating by the fire, she relished every bite. There was as chill in the breeze now, a clean, clear chill that she welcomed.

With the breeze came out her "trusted" wool sweater-the one she always wore because it always kept her warm. One of the matching sweaters she and Svein bought in Norway. His sweater remained in a dresser drawer never making it into the "Goodwill Bag." She just couldn't do it. After his death, she realized there are some symbolic things that are drenched in memories, some things that have a life of their own.

Now, thinking of his sweater, their days together, that trip to Norway, she put her hand on the coarse natural wool, opened her hand and touched a place over her heart. Again, she opened her hand, gently putting it in the center of her chest and felt again the soft wool. Tears began to flow from this small gesture and the wool absorbed the dampness.

Later, the flames of the logs dancing in the black night spit up at her. She watched as the wood consumed itself. One by one she fed the wood into the flames, re-read, and burned the months away-January, February, March, April.

A fleeting thought of how fast life slips away, much like the ashes in the fire before her. A worrisome thought that she's still waiting for the dreaded biopsy results and how life sometimes hangs in the balance, much like the unburned logs. She sighed. Then she remembered Kari going off to college to live away from her for the first time. Another deep sigh.

Nostalgically, she relived the setting up of the dorm room. She chuckled to herself at the pink and purple stuff crammed into her little car. Her night ended with gratitude for Kari-a smile thinking of her. She left a short message on her cell phone telling her that she loved her and would talk in the morning. Exhausted, she put out the fire, locked the car, and zipped the tent for the night.

Chapter Three

Although Ingrid often questioned the way she had grieved Svein's death, it seemed she grieved as appropriately and thoroughly as she could. The faculty at Loomis Chaffee, where she taught, understood at first but soon the talk in the teacher's room turned back to the classroom. Who was passing and who needed help! The parishioners at church were emphatic at first, but as the months passed they became involved in hiring a new pastor, Dr. Harrison Winslow. The calling, the interview, the excitement of his first sermon at Grace Lutheran.

Then, the church conversation around Ingrid became awkward. Slowly, the parishioners moved on; except for the support of her dearest friend, Carla. Ingrid felt out of place as she tried to fit in with them, except when she was with Carla, so she asked Carla to go with her to Dr. Winslow's

Installation Service. She even stood in line and dutifully greeted the new minister and his wife. Now, the scene flashed across her mind.

That morning of the new pastor's installation her cell phone rang just as she was getting out of the shower.

"Carla, yeah. I'm almost ready. I'll meet you in the parking lot."

Ingrid hurried so she wouldn't be late for the 10 o'clock service. As she pulled into Grace Lutheran, she saw Carla standing by her car. Carla, as usual in her "little black dress" and Ingrid wearing a neatly tailored bright blue suit with a colorful silk scarf. A gold lapel pin accented the bright blue and her gold loop earrings peeked out from behind her blond hair. She had no idea of the kind of first impression she left behind her.

The friends hugged briefly and hurried to the back door of the church. On the way into the vestibule, old Mrs. Edwards reached for Ingrid's hand.

"How are you, dear?" Mrs. Edwards's inquired, half in sympathy and half out of habit.

"I'm fine, Elizabeth, thank you." Ingrid smiled down at the older woman who seemed pleased to be able to reach out to someone familiar, someone who had cared for her, and someone she genuinely cared for. Even now, Ingrid stood out, even with no official role in the church. Her naturally blond hair stood out against the brilliant blue suit which fit her slender body perfectly. Svein had called her "his secret weapon" and always noticed that she didn't go unnoticed. He was always very much in love with her-for both her beauty and for her humble inability to see it.

Ingrid and Carla took their places in one of the middle pews as the choir sang, "How Great Thou Art." Shuffling through the hymnal, they joined in the singing. After the sermon, which wasn't in Ingrid's mind nearly as good as Svein's, Ingrid settled back to pray. Carla touched her hand as if to say, "This is hard." The former minister's wife smiled back knowingly and whispered, "It's OK."

At the end of worship, Carla and Ingrid joined the rest of the congregation as they stood at the back of the church forming a line to greet their new pastor and his wife. Harrison Winslow looked much like his sermon-dull and bound too closely to scripture-almost pale and without passion. He was short and balding and looked like he sent out his suit to the cleaners every week. His wife Magarita looked tired and matronly. She looked like she never sent out her suit to the cleaners at all.

"Good Morning, Reverend Winslow.   I'm Ingrid Mikkelsen. Welcome to Grace Lutheran."

"Hello, Ingrid, thank you. Thank you." In the crush of people, Harrison Winslow failed to acknowledge Ingrid's connection to his predecessor, Reverend Svein Mikkelsen. By the time he made the connection Ingrid was out of the church, and he had moved on to the next person. Another look from Carla.

Even after this difficult morning, Carla and Ingrid faithfully attended Grace Lutheran for several months. Then one Sunday at the coffee shop where the two friends always went after worship, Carla hesitantly offered, "What do you think about going to Asylum Hill Congregational in Hartford next Sunday?   Dr. Reed is supposed to deliver a great sermon."

Carla looked at Ingrid not knowing what kind of reaction she would get. Then, tried to soften her request with, "Just to try it." A bright smile spread across Ingrid's face. It was a sight that warmed Carla's heart. Strangely relieved,

Ingrid agreed to go on the very next Sunday. After that, they rarely went back to Grace Lutheran.

On her first morning at Sebago, Ingrid woke refreshed ready to explore. She zipped her tent, set out some fire wood for the night, grabbed a sweatshirt and headed for town. She knew exactly where she wanted to go. Yesterday, driving through Windham, Ingrid noticed a small gift shop called, "The Cry of the Loon". She remembered being there with Svein.

Now, as Ingrid drove up to the "The Cry of the Loon Shop", she noticed the carved ducks and loons in the windows of the barn. It took her away from her thoughts of school and church and back to the day she and Svein bought the carved loons for the cabin.

They put them on the fireplace in the great room of the cabin. That night they sat on the porch listening to the real cry of the loons. There was a strange solace, a strange sadness in their plaintive screams into the night. She loved the sound.

This morning as she looked around the shop, she noticed the colorful dish towels with loons, pictures of loons, all mixed in with the sweet fragrance of scented candle wax.

The scent reminded her of the quiet sensual nights in a soft canopied bed in their room at the back of the cabin. Her body missed the nearness of him most of all. Not just his touch, but especially the nearness. A soft familiar feeling stirred within her as she tried to remember what it felt like to be touched but the memory was distant. She shivered remembering the place where he stood by the door when he said, "Cry of the Loon. Catchy name!"

"Maybe we should get some "loony" stuff for the cabin," she countered. He took her hand as they went through the many small rooms. She sighed with the pleasure of having him all to herself, out from under the watchful eyes of the congregation.

"Do you like the blue or green ones?" she said holding up some small towels.

Svein was already preoccupied with the carved wooden loons on the window sill. They were lovely reproductions in black, white and green. He turned one upside down to check the price. Then, reluctantly set it down again.

"Let's get it, Svein! How much?" She looked. "69.95 and 49.95." He hesitated.

"They're so beautiful," she said as she quickly put the towels back. He sensed her excitement. Boldly he whispered, "Let's get one for you and one for me."

"Really?"

"Really."

Then he watched for that precious moment of childlike delight to envelope her face. He bought them. When they got back to the cabin, he placed the loons side by side on the mantel piece in the great room.

Later, when the sun went down, the cold night air crept up to the porch and covered them. She shivered. Svein noticed, "Sweetheart, let's move inside. I'll build a fire," he said touching her cheek. She leaned over to kiss him.

"I'll fill our glasses," she said as she took their glasses to the kitchen and poured the wine. Gathering up some blankets and pillows, she made a warm place near the fire. They snuggled examining the two loons perched on either side of the mantel.

These times were her favorite. No chance of late night hospital calls, no duty, no one else, just the two of them. He became her own. And she gave her whole self to these moments as they kissed by the fire.

"I adore you, you know," she said. He laughed not understanding she was telling the truth.

"And I love you, sweetheart."

Later under the down comforter, in their cozy bedroom at the back of the cabin, they explored each other's body and found special places that seemed elusive when in the correctness of the parsonage. Here they were able to express their desire in ways that seemed unthinkable at home. This was their soft place to fall-and spend themselves. They lingered long into the night just savoring the completeness of these moments together.

As she drove back to the campsite, she noticed that the traffic was light. Bob's Lobster Shack was completely empty. Only one car. I wonder how they stay in business. Probably closed all winter. Maybe Bob goes to Florida.

She felt a kind of heaviness inside. She kind of wished she bought something at the Cry of The Loon yet she knew she didn't need anything. She wished she had had something just as a reminder of being there. Her excitement to go there was to simply remember being there with Svein. To think about our memories here on the lake, and at the cabin.

Why is all this important? She chided herself feeling a little foolish. Maybe I'm a little crazy, retracing our steps, but I don't care. Somehow it prepares me for another school year. It's like if I don't do it, I won't be ready to go on. I need to go backwards so I can go ahead. A car in back of her blasted his horn as she turned sharply onto State Park Road. Her cell phone was buzzing impatiently.

"Mom, are you alright?" The anxious voice of Kari startled Ingrid back to reality.

"Sure, dear, I'm fine. Just took a little trip into town." Once her daughter was reassured, she described her junket to "The Cry of the Loon" with its endless "Loon" paraphernalia.

"It was definitely a "loony" place," she quipped. They laughed.

"I remember you and Dad took me there once. We got some dish towels for the cabin."

"Are you all settled in? How did the registration go?"

"Great, I got there early like you said and got the Western Civ with Henderson and English 101 with Dr. Angela Sander. A great teacher they say. Last night Ellie and Me went out for pizza with some guys from the dorm. It was fun. I think I'll like it here, Mom." Kari bubbled over with the excitement of a new found freedom.

Both mother and daughter hung on for a few minutes filling in each other with details, only hanging up when both were reassured the other was OK.

"We'll talk later," they both said at the same time. Then, they closed with the usual "love yous."

Later that day, the sun came up over Sebago Lake leaving bands of blue on the lake's surface. Darker strips were out near the horizon. By mid-day, the sun was hot and demanding, a welcome relief from early fog and cool shaded woods. Ingrid, now sitting on the beach, absorbed her surroundings with a healing peace. A lone loon was dipping into the clear water sometimes not reappearing for several minutes. Then, she noticed a pair of loons making their way across the lake. A black butterfly landed on her chair. She sipped her coffee and relished the moment.

Several times that afternoon she swam, steady and strong just like she had on her college swim team at Gettsburg College. Svein loved to see her compete because she had a physical edge and natural beauty. Others noticed her defined arms and legs, and tiny waist but she just took her body for granted.

Her beauty was never lost on Svein. Even the first time he saw her. "She took my breath away," he always told their friends. Because he was good with words, his wife never took his words literally, but figuratively. She was wrong. She did take his breath away.

On the day they met, she was sitting alone in the library. First, he noticed her blond hair. Then, her sharp blue eyes and white skin. A poster child for Norway-a delicate beauty.

"Pulling up his chair to her table, he asked, "Do you mind?"

"Not at all," she smiled and he was captivated by her. That was the moment he felt that he might not be able to breathe properly.

Ingrid, not wanting to show her interest in him, went on with her reading. He was taller than her with a rather square frame, dark curly hair and a boyish grin. She noticed his eyes were as green as the shirt he wore.

Settling down, Svein opened a large book in front of him. "Concordance" it said. Curious Ingrid watched him pour over the fine print inside. As he found the right quote, he would list it and write it on his paper. Then he crafted paragraphs around his quotes. Finally, she said, "I've never seen a book like that. What kind of research are you doing?"

At first, he searched for the correct answer but then, gesturing towards the thick black book, he offered, "Divinity School. I'm writing a sermon. This book helps me find the perfect biblical quote."

"Oh," she said looking back at her own literature book inscribed Greek Mythology. She gestured towards her notes answering, "Zeus, Neptune, Apollo and Venus".

"But not necessarily in that order!" he said smiling with his eyes, which was something he mastered a long time ago. She smiled back knowing they were as different as the two books they studied. She found that difference intriguing.

After that day, they found themselves together at the same table quite often until he caught his breath long enough to ask her out.

Wow, we were so naive and so young she thought. When Svein asked me to stay overnight, the night Benjamin was staying over with Dara, I could have been expelled. We were crazy in love.

It's amazing that we knew we'd be married some day. No question. Right after college. Everyone did. Didn't even debate it. Good thing my parents loved Svein because we 'd already decided by the time I graduated.

Ingrid remembered those early days as the sun of this perfect day in Maine drove her back into the water. The coolness enveloped her body as she dove in. It was biting and softly sensual at the same time bringing her back to this day.

But even in this peace, a familiar anxiety crept in. A conflict of not knowing how to let go but needing desperately to go on. Then, this fear of going on with the biopsy result pending. She had been here before. She had a need to share her worry and concern and a need to keep it to herself. A strong physical need to be touched and loved, a simple need to hold someone's hand, to touch toes in the night, to have a familiar conversation with a loved one. She needed someone to sip coffee with her in the morning.

After her swim, Ingrid fell asleep on the beach, face down on the sand. Her body was tired and in the warmth of the sun, she slept. She did not hear Derek pull into #148. When the sun started to dip down, she woke startled trying to remember where she was. As she gathered towels and beach bag, she noticed the RV next to her site.

"Darn, I was enjoying the solitude," she said softly. Then apprehensively she thought it's probably a family with kids and they'll be swinging on the swings all day. Then she saw the Mazda Miata convertible pulled up beside the RV and realized that # 148 would not be a family affair. A silent sigh of relief.

Ingrid decided not to set up a fire that night. Instead she went to Windham to grab a bite to eat and see a movie. She choose "Nights in Rodanthe", a simple love story with Harrison Ford and Diane Lane. At first, she related so much to Adrienne with her fear of relationship, of sexual contact, of reconnecting with a man.

Then, at the end she cried when Paul died. In fact, she sobbed uncontrollably. Like Adrienne who grieved at Paul's sudden death, she, once again, grieved Svein's death. The whole experience left her feeling empty and alone.

On the way back to the lake, Ingrid chided herself for taking on such a love story. Why do I do that to myself? She thought. Finally back at #149 where it was very dark, she rummaged around for her flashlight and picked her way to the picnic table. No one stirred in #148 - no lights or sign of life. Emotionally drained and physically tired, Ingrid quickly disappeared into the cocoon of her little tent. She snuggled into the silence and felt the immediate warmth of her sleeping bad. Finally, sound sleep!

Chapter Four

At 6AM, Ingrid could hear muffled sounds at the next campsite. Someone was trying not to make noise but making it all the same. Sounded like wood being stacked, smelled like a fire being lit. She turned over and went back to sleep. In time the smell of fresh brewed coffee, the pungent sweet scent of bacon seeped into the corners of her tent. By 7AM, she woke for good.

Getting undressed in such a small space was always a challenging task, even for an agile body that knew Yoga moves by heart. Once again, she had slept in her sweats. Now, she would find clean clothes and trudge over to the shower.

As she walked toward the grey black building that served as a bathroom and shower house, she noticed a tall, slender figure bent over the open fire cooking the old fashioned way-slabs of bacon and fresh eggs. A black porcelain coffee pot sat on top of the grate.

"Morning," she said as she hurried by anxious to reach the small grey building in front of her.

"Good Morning," he answered in her direction.

After she walked past Derek, the analytical school teacher in her shook her head in disbelief. What's he doing cooking like that when he has an RV? I don't get it. And he's alone? Seems unlikely. She's probably still asleep. But I suppose it's possible. I'm alone. She shivered in the cold morning air.

As the water from the shower touched her skin, she gradually warmed up. She let the shower head above spray her head and chest. The lower one warmed her lower body and legs.

Suddenly, the stream of warm water stopped. Not wanting to step out of the warmth, she pushed the cold steel "on button" again and again to avoid the inevitable "getting out." Finally, she wrapped her shampooed hair in a towel and faced the cold morning air.

As she dried her body, the towel scraped across a small bandage on her right breast. With no mirrors to remind her, she forgot to be careful as she pulled the towel back and forth over her shoulders and upper arms. As the edge of the towel scrapped against the bandaged place, she winced. Then reluctantly she remembered Dr. Bacon and her biopsy report.

This simple movement brought forth a torrent of powerful worries to her mind. Then she stopped herself. I'm not going to worry until there is something to worry about she thought. No, I have these hours, these days to relax, to be free from worry. I worried before and I was OK. I refuse to spend all my time dreading what may not even be real.

She finished drying her legs and feet. Her legs were thin, tanned and well defined. She had the body of "a fit Norwegian woman" Svein once told her. At the time "how she looked" was very important but right now all she wanted was a healthy body.

When Ingrid was seven years old her mother and father brought her from Norway to America. They immigrated to Gettysburg, Pennsylvania where there's a large contingency of Lutheran Norwegians. Several members of Hans Steepe's family came before him. The family found a community that was both welcoming and familiar.

After attending the local high school in Gettysburg, Ingrid Steepe went on to Gettysburg College. Excelling in her studies, she received an academic scholarship. When she met Svein, he was studying theology at The Lutheran Seminary in Gettysburg. Originally, his undergraduate work was done at Concordia College in Moorhead, Minnesota where his widowed mother still lived. His father had died of a massive coronary when Svein was just entering college.

Both Svein and Ingrid were only children; both were strong in their Lutheran faith. After their initial meeting in the library, both were very interested in each other. This interest and attraction grew throughout Ingrid's college years. Since Svein's mother was so far away, he adopted her family who lived on the outskirts of Gettysburg. By the time Ingrid was ready to graduate, she and Svein were planning a family wedding in the local Lutheran church.

Svein was interviewing for his first call to a parish and decided to start his service in the church back in Minnesota where he and Ingrid could be close to his mother. Kari was born in the cold of the Minnesota winter and provided warm company for her ailing grandmother. Several years went by until Mrs. Mikkelson passed away in 2000. Right after her death, Svein was called to The Grace Lutheran Church on

Woodlawn Street in Hartford, Connecticut. Four years later, he died in the parsonage from a massive heart attack leaving Ingrid and Kari alone.

There was no denying Ingrid's Norwegian background. Her blond hair, just like her mother's, had never darkened or faded. She had grown so used to people noticing her nearly white, pure blond hair that she no longer paid any attention to them noticing her. Sometimes women stopped her to ask where she had her hair done. Then she explained the Norwegian part.

Recently, she changed her hair cut to a nearly shoulder length straight cut. It could be dried in place. Riccardo, who had been her hairdresser for most of her adult life, knew exactly how to shape it so that people would continue to notice her.

Now, she slipped into her black sweat pants, the ones with the two white strips down the side. She pulled on a white shirt and zipped a snug fitting black jacket over her slender frame. Her make up routine was simple-some cream on her face and a dab of lipstick and she was ready for the day. Unassuming and unpretentious, she was unaware of how striking a figure she was.

Walking back to her campsite, she expected to see a woman emerging from the Flair RV but she didn't. The man had disappeared and the only thing that remained was the coffee pot on the grate, an empty chair and smoldering fire.

Later on the beach, Ingrid remembered her journals for the first part of the year. January, February, March, April, May and June. The re-reading gave her a sense of continuity. She recognized beneath her words a sense of loneliness. Every month seemed to run together. On January 20th, she wrote about her date with Josh who was newly divorced. He was the math teacher at Loomis and had asked her out right after the Christmas party. In February she wrote that she knew "it just wasn't working out." By March, she had conveyed that message to him.

At first it was awkward for them to try to be friends at school; but, by June, they had worked it out in order to co-exist in the same work space. Then there were the entries in February when she had the first biopsy. A lump discovered. How scared and alone she felt. And how relieved she was when it was benign. So easily removed.

Kari helped her through those days but Ingrid was changed after that. The experience made her want to live each day fully. She was ready to give up her loneliness, to commit, to love again. This trip to Sebago was an ending of sorts-the last commemoration of Svein and their life together. Ingrid's Lutheran background gave her a spirituality that grounded her. As she let the breeze wash over her body, she prayed silently that she might remain open and willing to what God had in store for her.

Then, she heard, "Beautiful day!"

"Yes," she said automatically. Startled out of her meditative state she looked up through the sun and saw the tall man from the early morning breakfast scene standing before her holding a cup of coffee.

"Would you like some coffee?" he offered sitting down cross-legged on a stump near her.

"There's plenty in the pot," he motioned towards the campsite.

"No, thanks. I had some juice and cereal earlier, but thanks for the offer."

"When did you come?" he asked.

"Last Tuesday. Just needed to get back to Sebago in the "off season". I try to come every year in September," she answered without fully explaining.

Derek sensed there was much more to her story-so much she didn't say.

"I know this is my favorite time here. I used to be a counselor over at Sunshine Camp when I was a kid. We always brought campers here to do some "real camping". I try to get back "off season" when I can but haven't been able to for a couple of years. Ingrid sensed there was something he wasn't saying as well, so she changed the subject to a lighter note,

"Real camping! So that's why the wood fire and coffee pot when you have a full kitchen." She smiled up at him.

"Yeah, the RV is great when it's raining but," he gestured vacantly toward the fancy rig and looked embarrassed at having to explain himself so Ingrid dropped the subject.

Suddenly, he stood up and Ingrid could see that he was muscular but a bit too thin for his frame. His coarse, wavy black hair had begun to grey not in any specific place but in sprinkles of white all over. The hair of a man graying prematurely. It didn't age him but made him more interesting. But there was something solemn, something terribly sad in his green eyes. She could always tell by the eyes where a person's been in life. A teacher's observation she noted to herself.

"Going to Aubuchon's in Windham to pick up some propane, and a newspaper. Do you need anything?"

"I'm fine," she said even though she knew she needed to pick up another heater for her tent. When he left, she thought I can't ask him to pick up a heater for me. I didn't even get his name. Don't think he even said it. Oh well, the old heater will get me through one more night.

Seems like a nice person but he looks really tired. Wonder why he's here alone. But I'm alone too. In a way it's nice he's here. He's a stranger but it isn't like I'm alone with a stranger. Old Mr. Pearson drives his golf car by twice a day. Other campers are here too. She looked towards #145 and #146. This is a public campgrounds. It isn't like I'm in the woods alone with this guy. But I don't think I'll mention him to Kari when she calls. She'll really start to worry.

For a moment, she felt almost apologetic. Then started to wonder why she felt it necessary to explain his presence even to herself. Was she interested in him? He seemed to be her age and eligible. But these thoughts were so foreign to her she dismissed them. She shook out the beach towels, gathered the rest of her things and retreated to #149 to make her lunch.

A cold front pushed in from the North so she dragged her chair down near the rocks in a protected place out of sight from the campgrounds. The wind whipped the dark grey water in even ripples as far as she could see. A single fisherman, trolling for trout, steered his row boat across the lake. A motorboat sped by unsettling the already choppy waters. The light blue sky, be speckled with white clouds, framed the picture. There she ate her lunch, read her books, and hugged the rock to avoid the brisk breeze.

Later in the day, when the cold breeze became uncomfortable, she retreated to build her campfire. Once again she pulled out her heavy wool sweater to keep her warm. This night she would need to spend by the fire.

Chapter Five

y the way, I'm Derek Holland," he said extending his hand over her fire. "I don't think I introduced myself earlier."

"Ingrid Mikkelsen. Did you get what you needed at Aubuchon's?"

"Yeah, all set for the night. Do you mind?" he asked as he pulled his chair over.

"Not at all," now she was glad for the company.

"Have you heard the weather forecast?" she asked.

"Cold front coming in tonight. Might go down into the thirties."

That was not welcome news to Ingrid but for now she was content. Somehow the sudden cold front didn't seem so important now that he was here.

"Have you ever vacationed in Casco or in the Sebago area," he asked.

"Actually, I used to camp here quite a bit-in a camp over on the other side of the lake."

"Did you sell it?" he inquired thinking she might give some background about herself. Her answer was entirely unexpected.

"No, it belongs to the Grace Lutheran Church Parish in Hartford, Connecticut." Seeing the puzzled look on his face, she added, "My husband, Svein, was senior pastor there for five years so we came as often as we could."

"Oh," He said not quite understanding but hesitating to ask if she was divorced. Again, she noted his puzzled look so she decided to just say it.

"Svein died suddenly. Two years ago. A massive coronary," she said looking away from the flames.

"I'm so sorry for your loss." He came back quickly with the words that seemed so limited but were always able to bring solace. He himself had heard them hundreds of times in the past eighteen months. He knew them well.

A few moments of silence passed between them. The fire was now beginning to take on the darkness of the night. It leapt up higher nearly spilling out of the self-contained fire ring. Derek put on another log after he retreated to the RV to get a bottle of wine from the Blacksmith's winery.

"Would you like to take a chance on this? I got it locally," he said holding up the wine bottle in the light of the fire. She laughed out loud recognizing the wine from her previous visits. Excitedly, she told the story of the time she and Svein found the winery by chance.

"We never drank much but that night, we drank the whole bottle. So, we ended up dancing the night away on the front porch. Svein loved to dance. The music was blaring away but no one called the cops." Then, her eyes lowered as she pulled back realizing she was talking to one man about another.

Derek noticed. "What's the matter?"

"I don't usually do that. Memorializing my dead husband with another man."

"It's OK. I understand. Really," his voice softened. "Where did he have the heart attack?" His question gave her permission to tell about coming home and finding Svein in the den- "asleep" in his black leather chair. After calling to him, she realized he was not responding. His color was grey, his body cold. At first, she was stunned but then she told him about her hysterical call to 911.

"I was screaming. My husband is not breathing. Come to 113 Woodbridge Road, Hartford. No he's not breathing. I think he's dead." Ingrid started to tear up remembering her panic and her pain. Returning to that moment was always the same. It overcame her every time even when she was sure she could tell the story without tears.

Silently, he refilled her glass as he filled his own. She motioned with her hand that that was enough. She went on with the story, "When the EMT's came, they tried CPR but couldn't revive him." A pause. "Massive Coronary! The autopsy verified that. He was just 50 years old. Ten years older than me. Just like that his life and mine were over," she said as she shrugged and regained her composure.

Derek listened without interrupting her. Finally, he said, "I'm so sorry."

"No, I'm sorry. I didn't mean to burden you with this."

"It's not a burden. I really do understand."

"Thank you," she answered looking directly into his dark eyes for the first time. Somehow her pain was mirrored there and it comforted her. For a few minutes they sat quietly.

Knowing she needed to lighten the mood and eat something to offset the wine she asked, "Are you hungry?"

"Starving."

"I have almost a whole left-over pizza in the cooler. Does that turn you off?"

He laughed, "Not at all. There's a microwave in the RV. I can heat it up in 2 minutes." Derek was happy to see that she had "pepperoni" which was his favorite. They shared the pizza on paper plates eating it as they sat by the fire. He found out that she taught at Loomis Chaffee and she found out that he worked for Morgan Stanley. She didn't ask why he was alone.

Then suddenly Derek quipped, "Now I know your age, 42 0r 43?" She just smiled at him without an answer. "I thought a woman never tells her age."

"You're exactly the same age as Jenny, my wife, five years younger than me. Ingrid's heart dropped as she heard him mention his wife. Where was she? Why was he here alone talking to her? She began to wonder about the wisdom of her being here alone with a stranger.

For his part, Derek was reluctant to talk about Jenny and Zack to a stranger but it came more easily once Ingrid revealed the death of her husband.

He explained, "Jenny died in a commuter train wreck just outside of Boston." The words were choked out of his throat. "Just 41. And Zack was seven. They were meeting me at a Red Sox game."

He turned away. Shocked, Ingrid turned towards him and blurted out, "I'm so sorry, so very sorry." She reached over to touch his arm. Now she understood the terrible sadness in his eyes. Again, they sat silently for a few minutes. Both saw the flames of the fire through the mist of a grief that was always with them ready to bring tears.

Derek explained how he received the call to come to the Mass General. How he couldn't believe what had happened and the haze of the early months after losing Jenny and Zack. He ended by expressing his anger at the publicity hungry media coverage that caused him such extended pain. Ingrid remembered the coverage and vaguely remembered stories of those who lost their life that day.

She shivered in the cold air.

When Derek saw her shiver, he quickly returned to the RV to get warm blankets. As he rummaged through the drawers in the bedroom, he thought about how much at ease he was with Ingrid. He knew instinctively that this meeting was a different experience for him. For a moment he remembered Britney, a woman from his office that he dated a couple of times. He could picture the bored vacant expression on her pretty face when he brought up Jenny or Zack. He remembered how she quickly changed the subject. She seemed offended by his sorrow. Then he thought of Linda, the divorcee who talked incessantly of her two children, ex-husband and divorce settlement. About six months ago Derek decided he'd rather be alone than endure such strained relationships.

But tonight was very different! Besides being beautiful, she understood. Secretly, he did not want this night to end.

"How long will you be here?" he asked.

"As long as the weather holds. I have a couple of weeks to myself right now. Kari, my daughter is off to college. It's a quiet time for me."

At first, he was startled to hear she had a college age daughter. Then when she told him she was only 23 when Kari was born, it all made sense. Jenny was 33 when Zack was born so somehow it didn't occur to him that some women in their forties might have kids in college. Both he and Jenny had spent their early years working on a career, not a family.

Ingrid's phone rang. Answering, she moved towards the beach.

"Mom, I've been trying to get you."

"I had the phone in my bag in the tent earlier. Sorry."

"Are you OK? I'm worried about you. Up there all alone."

"I'm fine, honey," she reassured her. "There are some other people here. I'm not totally alone," she said trying to calm the fears of her daughter but not wanting to explain Derek right now. Once reassured, Kari ran through a listing of the courses she signed up for, and some she couldn't get. Then, completely reassured she hung up quickly when her friends showed up to pick her up.

"Bye Mom, love you." With that Ingrid moved back to the warmth of the fire. "Sorry, my daughter's checking up on me."

"Usually, it's the other way around," he observed.

"Since Svein died we've been especially close. I think she sees I'm struggling," Ingrid looked at the ground, pushing the soft sand with her sneaker. "Ordinarily, I would never admit that to a stranger but it seems OK."

"I know," he said as a matter of fact. Again she knew that he really did know. Here was a man who was living her struggle. She told him that she felt more comfortable talking to him than any other man she dated in the last two years. He nodded his head in complete agreement. Then, they talked and laughed about some of their more interesting dating experiences.

The night air grew cold; the fire started to dwindle. They finished the night and the conversation over a cup of hot tea at the kitchen table in the RV. When Derek gave her a quick tour of the RV, she noticed the picture of his wife and child beside his bed. Silently, she wondered how anyone could endure the death of both spouse and child together-and such a beautiful wife and child. Her heart went out to him.

Actually, it took her breath away to see them. Still she did not prey with more questions.

Later that night as she fell asleep in the warmth of her little tent, she kept seeing the faces of Jenny and Zack. She dreamed strange dreams confused by feelings of loneliness, compassion, and desire, all mixed together. The next morning, when she woke, she knew her life was about to change

Chapter Six

The next morning, Derek dragged two lounge chairs and a small table down to the beach. Ingrid joined him and they relaxed in the sun, not really speaking but absorbing the warmth of being together. Derek decided to brave the cool water and swam while Ingrid rested in the chair on the beach.

At lunchtime, she filled a small cooler with sandwiches, pretzels, and soda. They walked through the park to a special spot that was away from the general campgrounds. There, on their "private beach", they ate lunch. After lunch, Ingrid swam out into the lake. He watched her, marveling at her clean even strokes and strong well-proportioned body. Ingrid was a woman of clean lines and natural beauty. There was a sensual strength in her movement. Her bathing suit was simple, black and perfectly fit to the contour of her body. What made her so beautiful was her inability to sense herself as "beautiful." She didn't bask in it. Her beauty just happened. That afternoon Derek noticed her beauty but he said nothing of it to her. It wasn't the time.

After her swim, they lay side by side and both fell asleep beside each other in the sand. There was little need for conversation that afternoon-the sound of the water, the softness of the wind, and the heat of the sun spoke for them.

Derek thought he missed talking to Jenny, sharing with her, playing with Zack but that afternoon he realized what he really missed was the comfort of silence. The moments of being together and not needing to speak. In some strange way, he realized he had rediscovered that comfort just by being with Ingrid, a woman who was, until two days ago, a stranger to him. There on that beach, now sitting quietly together, he knew he had found what he was longing for. She smiled at him. He smiled back. Neither spoke.

I don't think I can ever leave this woman he thought. But that's ridiculous! I barely know her. It's only been two days. I must be crazy even thinking this way. I can't do this! Not now! With my job falling apart. It couldn't be a worse time. How can I take care of someone else when I don't even know about my own future. I'm getting ahead of myself.

When they returned to the campsite, the weather shifted filling the sky to the brim with grey-white clouds, frothy whipped cream consistency clouds. Layer upon layer stretching out to the distant shore. There were crepe-like spacers in between where blue sky peeked through as dark grey masses hovered overhead. A storm-rain, thunder, lightning-and maybe some hail, the weatherman said.

A cold wind came in as dark clouds crowded out lighter ones pushing out the warmth. Then, in one moment, an opening high in the sky. The bright round disk of the sun was visible. Orange and light blue filmy fragments surrounded it as it pushed its light through. A moment of warmth. Would the storm pass them by? Then, full sun-delicious heat. As the storm clouds left like soldiers marching off to war, the sun found its opening to triumph in a clear blue sky.

"Amazing. We missed the storm," she said.

"I can't believe it. It passed right over us. Did you see how the dark clouds filled the sky? And the cold wind? But we missed it," he mused.

"And we both just stayed here waiting it out," she added overcome with the feeling of knowing something important had just happened, but not knowing exactly what.

He smiled and took her hand, "I'm glad we did!"

The rest of the afternoon was sunny with crisp linen-like clouds sneaking by the sun bringing no threats of rain, thunder or hail. It was a perfect September day at Sebago Lake.

That night by the fire, Derek told Ingrid about the train crash that took his whole family away in one day. At first, he talked about it as if it were a newscast on the local news. The commuter train on track three missed a signal, a massive accident, killing twenty five people and injuring 30. She listened quietly.

Derek put more logs on the fire. They watched as the flames consumed each other making delightful patterns that seemed to trip over each other. As he continued his accounting of that tragic day, his voice became deeper, softer-that of a husband and a father. She listened. Then his voice trembled when he said, "They asked me to identify the bodies."

Ingrid winced. A long pause. "I'm so sorry. So very sorry."

"I didn't want to see but I knew it was the last thing I could do for them. It was my final act of love." Softly, he cried. She did not interrupt him and he continued looking away.

"Jenny put her body around him-to protect him. Both were burned-black burned. Together," he motioned with both his arms. "I knew his Red Sox shirt-that was all. The position of her holding him and a small piece of a Red Sox shirt." Now, he held his hands over his face and openly sobbed. Deep wrenching sobs that punctuated the cold night air.

Crying herself, Ingrid moved to hold him close to her just as Jenny had held her son, cradling him in her arms. Neither one knew how long they stayed that way but in time his body quieted itself. The fire raged on as Ingrid's own tears fell on her warm wool sweater. Silently, she swept them away from the wool, now wet and damp, in the cool air.

Finally, Derek told her of the day he, impulsively, returned to the site of the crash and found a First Grade reading book in the bushes near the tracks. It was Zach's

Level One Reader with his name written in huge letters on the inside cover. He told her how he dropped to his knees in the grass hugging the book to his chest screaming, "No, No." Then, the tears came from him in a torrent of pain. Ingrid sat beside him crying quietly, until finally, once again, she held him against her warm wool sweater. When their tears caught the cool breeze, it sent a chill through them.

Derek felt her shiver. She looked at him seeing the deep sadness in his eyes. It was always there. Soon, he realized that the fire was dying now and they had to move.

"Will you come inside and sleep beside me - where it's warm?"

She straightened her back and pulled away.

"Beside me, not <u>with</u> me!" he said understanding her reservations but too exhausted to explain further. Then, understanding the simplicity of the invitation and of the moment, she said, "Yes, I understand. Yes, I will." Again, she shivered realizing how tired she was.

"Get your things, you'll catch cold," he told her.

As she quickly gathered her things and zipped her tent, she realized they both needed to sleep beside each other this night.

And that is what they did.

The next morning Ingrid looked up at the blue and white wallpaper on the walls of the RV. A predictable matching curtain hung from a valence over the window. At first, it startled her but then she remembered where she was. She felt Derek's presence in the bed even though they didn't touch and they were fully clothed. During the night she slipped off her heavy sweater sleeping in her sweats. Now the heater in the trailer whirred into gear.

He moved and she whispered, "Good Morning."

"I had the weirdest dream," he offered.

At first, she was afraid of what it might be. Then, she settled comfortably on her side listening. He put his hand on her shoulder and touched her lightly with his fingers.

"It was like everything was OK. Suddenly there was nothing to worry about. The price of gas was low again. The stock market didn't crash. There was no need to worry about anything. Everything was perfect. No Republicans, no Democrats, no presidential race. It just didn't matter. I kept looking around behind trees but nothing happened. Everything was OK-it was so easy," he said excitedly.

"Have you had this dream before?"

"Never, this was the first time. It was like I was "stress" itself and I was looking for "stress" but there wasn't any." She took his hand.

"I'm glad you had that dream."

"It wasn't like heaven or anything. Not in a spiritual way-no mist or like that. Just like it is here. Concrete things like trees and the lake."

"Was anyone with you? she questioned.

He frowned as he tried to remember then said, "There was a presence. Not a person really. But a presence. Maybe it was you. I don't know. I could feel a peaceful, easy presence."

"What a beautiful dream." They lay silently for a few minutes until the coffee pot began to gurgle like automatic coffee pots do.

"There," he said laughing, "easy just like the coffee."

She laughed and swung her feet over the side of the bed. She knew she needed to wash up and brush her teeth. She told him she would gather her things and go take a shower.

"You can use this shower," he offered.

"I'll be back soon," she whispered as she slipped out into the refreshingly crisp morning air.

That day they made breakfast together using her pancake mix and blueberries and his orange juice, bacon and coffee. The lake was clear as glass as they pulled their chairs to the water's edge and ate their breakfast. No one around except a few stragglers from the week-end. Soon, they too would be gone.

Derek pulled his chair closer to her. "Last night was so special to me." He felt like reaching out to touch her but hesitated. She took his hand.

"I know, for me too."

"It was a terrible week at work," he explained. "The market collapsed. All of us at Morgan Stanley are just hoping the company will survive. The team is apprehensive; the clients are calling full of fear. I came here totally discouraged and exhausted, and met you." He smiled.

She smiled back and then playfully added, "Now, everything is easy!" They both laughed. As he talked more about his work in terms she barely understood, she watched his face tighten.

"Have you checked in with your boss?"

"Thought I'd do that this morning. I just hate to switch my blackberry on. But I need to."

Sensing the urgency of his business, Ingrid found a solution.

"Listen, I have to go to town to pick up a new heater for my tent, just to have it." He looked at her quizzically not wanting to insist she stay with him another night. Perhaps she didn't want to.

"You do your work. I'll be back in a couple of hours."

After she left, he reluctantly returned to the world of subprime mortgages, stocks and bonds. Later, when he heard her car pull in, he cut his conversation with his boss short. It was almost as if the bad news that normally would worry him ran right over his brain. Abruptly, he stopped checking emails, and stopped texting. Today he was determined to use every minute he had "just feeling easy."

Chapter Seven

Ingrid was at the picnic bench struggling with setting up her heater when Derek came outside. She looked up happy to see him. There was something different about his expression, almost mischievous.

"Want to have some fun?" he asked with a hint of impulsivity in his voice.

"What do you have in mind? I'm easy!" she countered closing the box containing the heater. It snapped shut in one easy motion.

"The Fryeburg Fair. I saw it on TV. We could make it up there today. Have some corn on the cob, hot dogs. Have you ever been?"

"Years ago. But I'd love to! I'll get my jacket and purse." As Derek retreated into his RV to get a map in case the GPS failed, Ingrid retrieved her things from the tent, tidied up the site and locked her car.

Once in the tiny Miata, Derek set the GPS for Fryeburg as she settled into the seat beside him. She noticed how his hands curved around the steering wheel; how sure he was that the car would react to his touch.

She thought about how good it felt to be sitting beside him. Just to be "going someplace" with a man. Funny how you don't miss some little thing until you do it again she thought. To belong with someone, to be part of a couple. I can't think that way after two days but it feels like we're a couple.

Driving out of the state park, the coarse dark green pines crowded in on the road like soldiers in uniform. She noticed the signs that marked sections of the park not being used during "off season". Looking deeply into these areas, she saw cold, damp and dark unused acreage waiting for the winter snow. "Do Not Enter."

Suddenly a sadness came over her. More than a sadness-a realization. Since Svein died I'm like those restricted places she realized. Closed up! Just folded into myself! Actually cut off from myself. No feelings. Just existing with dark and damp places that have signs saying "Do Not Enter." She shivered.

"Are you cold? I can put the top up."

"No, I'm fine. Just fine," she smiled as she moved closer to him. Again the warm feelings. She could feel her body next to his. She purposely did not move away but absorbed his warmth.

He felt her move closer to him as they drove through Bridgton. It was comforting but strange. It had been so long since he welcomed any kind of closeness. Almost as if it were a betrayal of Jenny. In his mind he knew it was a crazy thought but in his heart he still felt unfaithful. Sometimes he wondered what he was being unfaithful to until one day he figured it out-her memory. The memory of being a couple, a family. Somehow that had now been erased from his heart.

In Bridgton, Derek noticed the Flower Bed Farm Antiques store and The Cool Moose. Might be fun to explore sometime he thought. He remembered how Jenny loved the antique stores and going to Reny's when they camped on the Saco River. They were there canoeing when Zack was just five. That was the time they bought the maple desk that she had refinished for the hallway in Hingham, he remembered.

Flashes of Jenny and Zack came up like a Power Point presentation. Quick mental shots of Jenny's smile, the way she moved so quickly when she was excited. The way she held Zack's hand as they crossed the street. Memories from past visits crowding now into his mind. He looked at Ingrid as if to get some relief from these images.

She's different from Jenny. Quiet like now, but not shy. Kind of peaceful. When she moves it's always smooth, deliberate. He noticed how her blond hair framed her face and how she never wore more than a trace of red lipstick. She was always busy but never rushed. Jenny was a whirlwind of action, chatter and ideas. She wouldn't leave the house without make-up. Actually, Derek was relieved that they were so different. Like, not really replacing Jenny, he thought.

"I wonder what that lake is?" she asked pulling him out of his musings.

"Kezar Lake. I think," he answered.

"I believe Fryeburg Academy is just beyond here. Loomis Chaffee sometimes competes with them in the New England Drama Festival," she added. When she saw the red brick buildings of the campus she told him about her trip there with her class. They both watched as the classic stately campus unfolded before them.

"There's something majestic about these New England Prep Schools", she commented. He noticed how her face lit up when she talked about her school work.

"Do you like your work?" he asked.

"Love it. It's been my life since Svein," she said without reservation. She went on to explain how the congregation let her stay in the parsonage for six months while she finished her Master's Program in Classical Studies.

"Where you ever afraid that teaching Latin and Greek might leave you limited as far as employment?" the investment broker asked as if by rote. She answered simply, "You do what you love."

Her answer seemed complete in itself so he didn't dare respond.

Seeing Fryeburg Academy with its impressive brick buildings and large open courtyard, reminded Derek of his days at Lawrence Academy in Groton, Mass. His mother and father sent him to board at the school when he was 15. This was a decision that he hated at the time but came to appreciate in time.

Both of Derek's parents were in their late thirties when he was born. As an only child, his life was lonely but privileged. They belonged to Vesper Country Club in Tyngsboro, played golf there and owned a summer home on Cape Cod. His father John Holland owned Holland Woollen Mills in Lowell, Mass where they lived. All he knew as a child was the stately Victorian home on Andover Street, having Christmas and Thanksgiving dinner at Vesper and attending a private school.

Secretly, he envied the neighborhood kids, the local ones who went to the Peter Reilly Elementary School down the street. From his bedroom window he could see them coming back from school, pushing and shoving and fooling around. He watched as they crossed busy Andover Street and retreated down Thorndike Lane to their small box-like colonial houses.

Derek was always close to his parents and rarely had a disagreement with them. As they got older, they found the harsh, cold winters of New England too difficult to bear and moved to Asheville, North Carolina. Now they were able to golf all year long in their retirement condo right on the golf course. Soon they made friends and established a new life.

After Derek graduated from Cornell, he married Jenny. They would visit his parents every year. When Zack was born, his mother came north for a couple of months to help out and grew very fond of Zack. Each summer the grandparents would come north to spent time with them. All grew as a family through the love of the grandchild.

After the tragedy struck, Derek made the effort to visit in the first few months but then he had to pull away. It was almost as if their immense grief intensified his own. Making his job his life seemed natural because he knew if he didn't stay consumed with something, the sadness of his own life would consume him. These past two days were the only break in his life for many months. It seemed strange but welcome.

Chapter Eight

As soon as they parked in the open field near the fairgrounds, they heard music blaring from the opening gate. Then, a woman's voice, "Welcome to the Fryeburg Fair. Have a wonderful day!"

After getting tickets, Ingrid and Derek walked together down a well-trodden path, past the "Cliff Hanger" ride, which looked ominous, and then, straight into the barn with the sign "Show Horses".

"We'll see some beautiful horses here," she said enthusiastically. Since she was a child in Norway, she always loved horses. It brought back memories of riding bareback with her cousins.

As they walked from stall to stall, she marveled at the majesty of these beautiful animals, so enormous and so powerful. Some stood perfectly still; some nibbled at bunches of hay hung appropriately to the side of the stall. In a small space near the stall, their proud owners had hung bright blue, yellow and red rosettes of 1st Place, 2nd Place and 3rd Place.

"It's a whole other world," he noted.

She agreed with a nod and continued to absorb this moment. Seeing this world again took Ingrid from her small human concerns, her grief, to the majesty of nature. It was a welcome shock to her sensibilities as childhood memories, buried deep inside, began to surface. She felt alive again.

These horses, so majestic. So full of power and beauty she thought. A black Andalusian reaching out to her. She responded immediately touching the full crest of his neck. He nuzzled her and she laughed. Just that touch brought back her childhood memories of Norway and Mr. Gentry, a horse she rode as a child.

When they emerged from the barn, the tangy country music of the "Fryeburg Fair Boys" greeted them. It was Hank Williams at his best. They sat on a bench listening to "Your Cheating Heart" and "You Are My Sunshine'.

Derek smiled down on her enjoying her and the energy of the music with its sometimes on key and sometimes off key unbalanced presentation. What it lacked in perfection, it made up for in energy. It was lively. Both enjoyed the happiness of the moment.

The energy of the music reached Derek. This is what I've been missing. Just having fun he thought. A simple song, sitting quietly, peacefully here. All foreign to him these days. It was almost as if having fun was a long distant memory that he dared not resurrect. Again he wondered how much of life he was missing just by not "daring" to.

"I'm so glad we came," he said.

"Me, too."

"Are you hungry?" he asked as he pointed to the candy apples, cotton candy, popcorn and ice cream that awaited them. Right in front of them there were dozens of booths lined in rows to the left or right. Taking out the little map of the fairgrounds, they decided to venture down the main aisle.

"We'll check out the 'goodies'."

"Look there's cotton candy."

"If I start on that I won't eat anything good for me," she said.

"And corn dogs. Sausage rolls. Popcorn."

"Stop it," she answered playfully punching his arm. He put his arm around her squeezing her to him. She felt good-like she fit with him. They walked like that all the way down the main row of booths debating their choices until they found a small seafood place at the end of Expo One.

"A lobster roll. How could I come back to Maine and not have a lobster roll?" She had decided. He had clam chowder in a bread bowl. They sat at a picnic table eating their lunch as the Blue Willow Band belted out its soulful country music.

Ingrid noticed how relaxed Derek had become since they entered the fairgrounds. She felt it too. It was as if they entered a different world of farmers, livestock, and crafts. A simple life.

"I'm so glad we did this," she said once again toying with the idea of saying how wonderful it was to feel alive again, to be together doing something as simple as having a lobster roll at the Fryeburg fair-but she held back.

Derek was different from Svein. Younger, darker. He didn't have the reserved nature of someone who had been trained as a minister. She liked the spontaneity, almost impulsiveness, for a change. Even though she never really seriously thought of anyone since Svein. Now she was opening the door to an easier relationship.

After lunch they strolled through the crowded aisles stopping to look at hand knit scarves and hats in the Fiber Center. She put on a fluffy white angora beret but hesitated at the eighty-two dollar price tag.

"Try it on," he coaxed her. When she put it on, it accented her blond hair and fair skin. Her blue eyes stood out even more. Perfect for her he thought. However, not wanting to spend that much she quickly removed it and moved on through the even more expensive alpaca sweaters and scarves.

"That hat was perfect."

"Too expensive, Derek," she replied with a resolve that showed her practical side. He appreciated that but later when she went to the Ladies Room, he went back to the Fiber Center, bought it, and stuffed it into his jacket pocket. After he bought the hat, he thought about his job wondering how much of anything he'd be able to afford if he were laid off. He shrugged it off thinking I really needed to get that hat for her.

In the Ladies Room, Ingrid checked her phone and saw she had several missed calls from Kari. She dialed her number.

"Hi, Mom. I've been trying to call you. Are you alright?" Kari said after picking up on the first ring.

"I'm fine honey. I just now saw that you called. I'm at the Fryeburg Fair. I'm finally able to get reception. The phones are a little "iffy" at the campground."

"What are you doing at the Fryeburg Fair?"

"Just something to do for the day," her mother told her as she explained the horses, the rides and the food. "It's been fun, getting out seeing people, doing something different." For now, Ingrid did not mention Derek knowing that information would cause Kari further worry.

"Ok," Kari said satisfied that her mother was alright. Then she launched into a quick summary of her first impressions of UConn, and her new friends. The excitement and happiness was evident in her voice.

"It's so much fun."

"We'll talk some more later," her mother said not trying to put her off but knowing Derek was waiting for her.

"Bye, Love you, Mom.

"Love you too."

Back with Derek they walked along side by side. Then, almost by accident, they drifted into the "Pulling Arena" where the open pulling contests were taking place. They had to climb through the crowd to the very top of the bleachers where they could see. Beautiful heavy strong black, brown, grey and beige draft horses were brought in two by two to pull 500 hundred pound concrete blocks. The blocks, piled two by two, had more weight added as the contest went on. The owners were announced by a Mr. Hall, the ring master. The track was raked and groomed by his sons.

Ingrid and Derek felt as if they were voyeurs looking in through the window of a world they barely knew existed. The old man with the Maine drawl talking about his livestock, the young boys in overalls walking behind their father helping to direct the horses. The handlers of the animals yelling and whipping their backs, flicking the whip near their faces and switching their legs and feet. The shear brute strength of both animals and men.

"This is unbelievable," Derek said more to himself than anyone. Then, he whispered to her, "Pretty far removed from my world of Morgan Stanley, the bail-out package, and the banking world."

"And my world of Greek mythology and Latin. I was just thinking that what I do in the classroom seems so important to my students and their parents. GPA, the SATS, National Honor Society-that stuff! What college? Will it be Ivy League?" She laughed.

"Not exactly like Fryeburg Maine and the Horse Pulling Contest," he added.

"Coming here makes me realize that there are many levels of achievement-like winning first prize in the Horse Pulling Contest. There's another real, visceral world out here!"

As they left the pulling contest, Derek shared his thoughts with her. He told her that this visit showed him that there are some very real people, like farmers, relying on banks to run their business, to feed their animals. Some real people using credit to buy tractors and farm equipment. Lately, his business life had been encased in a mountain of technology imprisoning him by keeping him within reach of his computer, phone or blackberry. This day was real for both of them.

Later that afternoon, when Ingrid refused to ride "The Cliff Hanger" because she was sure she might lose her lunch, he convinced her to ride on the Ferris wheel instead. Not once but twice.

When they reached the top, he put his arm around her and watched as her blond hair went flying out behind her head. Again, she snuggled close to him. As she did, she realized they fit together perfectly. Being 5 foot 8 inches had never been a problem for her because she loved being tall. But now she was glad Derek was 6 foot 3 inches. Warm sweet feelings came to her.

When the Ferris wheel stopped abruptly at the top, it jolted the carriage. She lurched backwards. He leaned over and kissed her lightly on her forehead. There was something innocent, and incredibly appropriate about that first kiss–at the top of her head, at the top of the world on a Ferris wheel at the Fryeburg Fair.

As the day wore on, more and more people came to the Fair. The aisles became narrow, crowded with teens and families with strollers. Derek held her hand tight so she wouldn't get separated from him. He tried to win a stuffed animal for her but finally gave up in frustration. They went through The Fun House.

"In honor of Halloween. Soon it will be Halloween," he said convincingly. Fun Houses were not for her but somehow he made everything exciting. Inside, they clung together as she hung onto him when she was confused, screaming, or just plain scared. They emerged laughing like children.

"That was hysterical," he said as they made their way back to the campsite.

Chapter Nine

It was dark when they arrived back at Sebago. Derek lit the lantern, got some logs for the fire, and retrieved more comfortable lounge chairs which were in the storage compartment under the RV. He pulled the chairs close to the fire as Ingrid unfolded two blankets to wrap around themselves as they huddled by the fire. Even though the September air had turned cold enough to be a sharp reminder that winter will eventually come, the warmth of the fire offset it.

"This is luxury."

"Being with you is luxury," he answered giving her permission to tell him about how she felt about the whole day-in the car, holding hands, and riding on the Ferris wheel." He nodded smiling as she spoke.

"Oh, speaking of luxury, I almost forgot," he said as he took the white angora hat from his pocket and handed it to her.

"You didn't? When did you? I can't believe it." Immediately, she pulled the hat onto her head with the contents tags flapping in her face. She smiled happily and struck a pose like a model. He knew then he had made the right choice.

"I love it. But I knew it was too much. How did you know I loved it?"

"It's perfect on you. I couldn't let it go. So, I went back while you were in the Ladies Room."

She pulled away from him in a pretense of indignation but then leaned forward and kissed him. It was a kiss that was smoldering in her all day, ever since the Ferris wheel kiss. He welcomed it feeling the soft angora against his face, loving the way she felt near him.

Still holding her, he whispered, "I know we just met a couple of days ago," and then, he hugged her tighter, "there's something special here." His voice trailed off.

"I know," she whispered not really knowing what she was agreeing to but responding more to the feelings of the moment than the words she heard. As he settled back in his chair he momentarily thought of Jenny; she hesitated thinking of Svein. For several minutes they sat in silence until he noticed the fire getting low. He reinforced it with more wood. It warmed them again. They kissed again.

The evening went on as they shared their feelings about this magical day. Then, the evening chill became too much for the fire's warmth. Then, he, noticing how cold it was, ventured, "Sleep beside me-it's too cold for you out here tonight." She looked at her little tent and the propane cartridge that needed to be attached to the heater.

Not wanting to ruin what they had together, she answered truthfully. "It's too soon for me to sleep <u>with</u> you but I will sleep beside you. Are you sure you're OK with that?"

As he remembered the picture of Jenny and Zack on his bedside table, he was slightly relieved. Then, in a lighter tone, he joked, "Remember what I said yesterday, 'everything is easy,'" He laughed and gave her a little kiss on her head much as he had done on the Ferris wheel. She laughed, convinced again by this very simple gesture. She went to her tent picked up her nightgown, bathrobe and toilet case as she jogged over to the shower.

First, she let the warm water rush over, then dried quickly in the cool air and hurried back to the warmth of the RV to sleep beside him. When Ingrid opened the door of the RV, she could smell the scent of a man's cologne. It was a familiar scent-one she hadn't known for some time.

Propped up in bed, he had turned down one side for her. She slipped into the bed and snuggled next to him. The picture of Jenny and Zack were there on the night stand. She looked away.

"<u>Beside</u> not with, OK?

"I told you, I'm easy." They laughed at the same time which broke the tension. Now, she had so many questions–were his parents alive? What about his childhood? What about hers?

She had no idea he had traveled to Norway. He had visited her home town. Now describing it as she remembered it. He talked about his loneliness as a child and his relationship with his parents.

Ingrid talked about Kari and how concerned her daughter was about losing her last parent. She explained how she had called her today just to let her know where she was and that she was OK. She explained how close they were as a family and how supportive Kari had been last winter when she had the cancer scare.

She decided to confide in him as she had not done before, "there was a biopsy. It was benign. But there is something more, I'm waiting for a second biopsy. Will know in a few days," she touched a place on her breast where the small bandage was hidden by her nightgown. He could see she was uncomfortable talking about it. Almost as if she feared he would reject her. He reassured her, "I'm glad you told me. I had no idea."

Then, trying to reassure herself she added, "I'm sure it will be fine-just like it was before." When she saw the softness in his eyes, suddenly she began to cry. For a man who had recently identified his wife's broken burned body, there was little personal alarm with more ordinary every day dilemmas. But he did respond to her obvious fears and held her close reassuring her.

Finally, exhausted from the newness of the feelings of the day, he turned off the light. The picture of Jenny and Zack were no longer visible, and they drifted into a deep sleep.

The next morning Ingrid slipped out of bed leaving Derek still enveloped in that deep sleep. She knew he needed sleep so, finding her journal, she made her way to the beach. Because there were so many feelings bombarding her, she was desperate to have the space to write and process those feelings.

She noticed the ribbons of dark blue touching the light blue sky as the water filled the bay. The waters were choppy. The light white and grey formations of early morning clouds hung overhead. Off in the distance, a lone motorboat was making its way along the shore. A treed island interrupted the clean lines of the shore. Eagles were circling their habitat-a protected haven. The silence was broken by the plaintive cry of the loon.

Kari called around 9 o'clock, just before her first class. "Hi Mom. Just wanted to check to see how're you're doing this morning and that you made it back from Fryeburg. I'm on my way to class."

"I'm fine dear. Just waking up. It's really relaxing here and the weather is nice, too."

"Any plans for the day?"

"Not yet," her mother answered truthfully yet knowing she would tell her about Derek at another time. Finally, Kari had to run to class so Ingrid avoided any difficult moments.

Returning to her journal, Ingrid wrote of her need for connection with Derek and of her fears, her hesitancy about the biopsy results. She wondered if she should have told him so much. But it seemed right. It all seemed so right. A sense of urgency came over her. Again, the cry of the loon pierced the silence speaking to her of the transiency of life and her need to be connected, to share a loving moment, not tomorrow but now. Tomorrow might not come.

Her confusion, her delight, her needs all spilled out on the page. She knew she needed to be with him physically. Next time she would take a chance. Next time, if there is a next time, she would sleep with him and not next to him.

Chapter Ten

It was nearly noon when Derek finally emerged. He looked relaxed, clean shaven. Not nearly as tense as he had been the day before.

"I didn't want to wake you. You were sleeping so peacefully," she said kissing him on the forehead and hugging him warmly. He held her in that hug for a long moment.

"I didn't mean to sleep away the day," he said smiling at her, "but I'm glad to be able to sleep like that. This was the first peaceful sleep since … well, you know," his voice trailed off not wanting to return to a sad place.

"Yes, I know," she changed the subject by handing him a mug of coffee.

"Made it on my little Coleman," she announced sitting close to him on the picnic bench.

"Norwegian style?" he teased delighting in her obvious pride in her accomplishment.

"Yah! Norwegian style." She smiled back. This time he kissed her lightly on the mouth and hugged her as if he had found something precious and couldn't let it go.

Then, holding her out from him with his hand encircling her waist, he whispered, "I have a surprise for you-are you up for another exciting day?" he asked as he finished his coffee.

"Sure, I'm easy," she quipped.

"Ok, off to Naples," he said not letting go of her but leading her in the direction of the car. She quickly grabbed her purse as he locked the RV. They left the nearly vacant park and headed for the highway.

The trees were just beginning to change colors - orange, rust, red and yellow. The fall colors mingled with the green pines. As they headed out to 302, they discovered that the Songo Lock was open letting a boat pass through.

"Look, he's turning the bridge by hand," Derek said in amazement. To the left side of the wooden bridge a man stood holding a crank in his hand. He walked in circles. The bridge responded and slowly came back in place.

"Wow, that was different!"

"Only in Maine," they said in unison looking at each other. Ingrid laughed pushing her blond hair back with her hand. Derek noticed her natural beauty. She was different somehow. When she first explained that she was from Norway, he understood.

In 1995, when he traveled to Oslo, Norway on business, he was captivated by the beauty of the blond fair-skinned Norwegian people. Every time he stole a look at her, it reaffirmed his original assessment.

She's so beautiful he thought. I love to look at her. It's the same as it was in Norway. Just clean natural beauty, much like the country. Then he realized that Ingrid's face was the first woman's face he felt compelled to memorize. Since Jenny that is. For a moment he felt the joy of that sense of appreciation, that kind of attachment to a beautiful woman, the excitement of it all. There was a strange comfort in his observations but also a slight sense of betrayal and confusion. He battled those feelings now.

When they got to Naples, Derek suggested another lobster roll and clam chowder. Since Ingrid had completely neglected breakfast, she was famished and couldn't resist.

They pulled into Sally's Flight Deck Restaurant, a typical Maine restaurant with a screened porch and a dining room jutting out near the water.

Once inside the dining room, with its dark wood and beige linoleum flooring, Ingrid asked for a table overlooking the lake. They watched as the sea planes taxied in dodging the motor boats. Clearly, the attraction to Sally's was right outside the windows.

"Look at this," he pointed to a small card on the table. "Black Fly Coffee. Dark and strong." He feigned disgust at the name. "Are you game?"

"I'm easy," she said with a coy smile that indicated she was flirting with him. Her tone surprised her so she blushed and drew back to a more conservative place, the place of Svein's wife, a proper minister's wife.

"Why not, coffee is always good," she continued to offset her more daring remark. Derek noticed her struggle and simply took her hand. Then they ate their lobster rolls and chowder with the obvious delight of two people who hadn't been in Maine for some time.

"Delicious. But the coffee was a disappointment.

"Too dark and strong," she whispered, "no matter how much cream I put in, it's still is too dark and strong." They looked forlornly at the dark liquid there in their cups. At that moment Ingrid began to laugh out loud. Much like she does when she's with Kari. Always, when they run into impossible situations, they laugh.

Now, he saw the humor in their impossible coffee. He poured all the cream into it; they laughed some more. Still, the coffee remained black. Finally, after they asked for more cream and several more tries and more laughing, they gave up on it and left.

On the pier outside Sally's, they watched the Naple's seaplanes taking off and landing. Then, Derek divulged his secret. Watching her face, like a little boy giving a gift to his Mom, he said, "I booked a flight for 2 o'clock."

"You're kidding."

"No."

"That's why you were looking at your watch in there," she said leaning into him pretending to hit him in the chest.

"We're on schedule. Here comes Bill Ross, the pilot," he said motioning to the trim, tanned man heading up the dock.   Then he whispered to her that he saw his picture online.

After Bill introduced himself and got them settled in the plane, he yelled out over the noise of the motor, "Where to?"

"Out over Sebago Lake to Sebago State Forest," Derek yelled back.

Once on their way, they held hands as they lifted up over the luscious green and multi-colored tapestry unfolding below them. The blue water blended with the colors as if woven with the delicacy of a master craftsman.

"This is beautiful, exciting," Ingrid shouted. Her blue eyes became even bluer in the excitement of the moment. Now, he was glad he had thought to go online to set this up, to surprise her. Suddenly, he felt alive and as vibrant as she looked.

"Sebago Lake, Sebago State Park," Bill said as he pointed down.

They strained to see site # 148 and 149. At first, the RV was lost under the trees but then as they circled Derek shouted.

"There we are! See! See! There's the Flair and your car. And that little dot is your tent." The pilot looked at Derek not understanding.

"Never mind." Derek motioned aimlessly towards Bill knowing he couldn't understand the situation. They laughed again delighted to have found their own little spot. The only place they could call their own. As they moved south of the campgrounds, Derek pointed out The Sunshine Camp where he worked as a teenager.

"There's the pavilion, the dock."

Ingrid watched it all with wonder, almost a giddy feeling. She loved his sense of surprise and adventure. It brought out a newness in her-a lightness, dormant since her youth.

After the ride they went on to Main Street in Bridgton and poked around in the Corn Shop Trading Company. Then moved on to The Flowerbed Farm Antiques Store. They ambled lazily through every nook and cranny commenting on this hutch or that table. She was surprised he knew so much about antiques.

"You ask the right questions," she observed after they left the second musty little shop.

"Jenny was an antiques nut," he explained.

"So was Svein. My style is more Danish modern but I love looking."

They stopped at The Laughing Moon Boutique, where Ingrid got a colorful shirt for Kari, and on to The Little Mountain Country Store where they got ice cream. His sundae was elaborate with mixed flavors; hers, simple, easy. Strawberry ice cream with fresh strawberries and whipped cream. Over ice cream they talked about how easy it was to share with each other.

"I don't know why but I don't have to hold back with you. To be careful that I don't mention Jenny or Zack. You know?"

"Or me with you."

Then, he hesitated wondering if he should say what was in his mind.

"I have been thinking about your test. I need you to know that I'm glad you told me.

"I wondered," her brow wrinkled as she frowned trying to hide her anxiety. He sensed it.

"You can tell me anything," taking her hand he waited until her face softened and she looked up at him. Leaning into her, looking directly into those blue eyes, he continued almost in an intense whisper, "We are here now. This is all I have. Today. Losing Jenny and Zack taught me that."

"I know," she whispered.

"You're alive and well today, Ingrid. That's all that counts with me." She held his gaze for a few minutes and squeezed his hand letting him know she understood.

"Thank you for saying that." Then, feeling a sudden relief, calmness swept over her. It was one of those times when she didn't know how anxious she'd been about his response to the possibility of her having a serious health problem-breast cancer. Her own mother died of breast cancer so she knew it's power. Yet she knew it was always better not to lie by omission. After all, it wasn't as if they were married for years. She had just met him. She hadn't even been intimate with him. Of course, it bothered her. Now, he made his response perfectly clear.

"When someone you love dies, it gives you a deeper appreciation for each moment of life," he concluded.

"I feel the same way," she added holding his hand even more tightly. "For today, I am well, I am here with you and everything is 'easy'." She laughed as she played with their favorite word.

When they got back to #149, Ingrid texted Kari to let her know she was alright. Her daughter was in the library studying so she appreciated the quick text and told her mother they would talk tomorrow.

It had started to rain. Not a drizzle but a steady cold rain that made the whole campsite soggy. Even the box from the new heater which Ingrid left on the table, was wet.

"You can figure this out tomorrow," Derek said as he put the soggy box under the trailer. "Let me make you some tea and pie."

On the way home they stopped at Dingley's Farm to buy a fresh blueberry pie. Once inside the RV, Derek found a towel to dry Ingrid's damp hair, and put on the kettle.

When she moved across the kitchen to get cups for the tea, he moved quickly toward the frig for the milk. The carton was slippery and flew out of his hand. Ingrid gathered some paper towels as he took a dish cloth from the sink.

As they wiped the floor, he noticed how her shirt fell open to reveal her breasts. There was a small bandage there. Putting his hands on her forearms, he gathered her to him.

Last night, when she told him of the biopsy it was clear to him, but now seeing the bandage made the possibilities more real and made her more vulnerable, more precious.

They kissed while the milk ran in a steady stream into the corners of the small kitchen, even under the refrigerator. Slowly, he removed her shirt and kissed all around the small bandage.

"Ugly," she whispered.

"No, you're beautiful, alive and real-with me, here and now."

Tears came first and a passion that emphasized her vulnerability and his need. The bedroom was darkened so they could not see the picture of Jenny and Zack. He felt free, unhampered by the past and she felt free, unafraid of the future.

They experienced each other's body with an abandon that was forged out of many hours of being alone and feeling untouched. Now, they returned to all that had been sensual, familiar to them. Familiar, even though it was not Svein, or Jenny. He returned to the curve of her breasts, the softness of her skin; she, to the touch of his hands, and the firmness of his body. Both to their deep desire to satisfy each other.

They did that. Finally that rainy night, relief from pain. Grief was lifted, wounds began to heal. They slept in each other's arms until slivers of the morning light crept in between the curtains.

Chapter Eleven

That morning Derek left early without waking Ingrid. She slept with a determination she had not known since Svein died. A peacefulness permeated every cell of her body leading her in and out of dream sequences. The only other time she remembered that kind of sleep was after running a marathon-a healing drugged sleep without the drug.

When she finally woke, she realized that the picture of Jenny and Zack was there on the bed stand looking down at her. It didn't upset her because she knew they belonged there. No more unease. Derek is who he is and they were part of him.

It was nearly ten o'clock. Since he'd left a clean towel and fresh bar of soap on the counter, she decided not to go to the public shower this morning. It was small but warm and cozy in his shower. After she took her shower, she made her way outside. The screen door squeaked after her but Derek was not within hearing distance. Then she saw him standing over a red canoe pulling it up on the shore. He waved for her to come see.

"They let me borrow it over at Sunshine Camp."

"You're kidding. What are you going to do with it?"

"Explore the lake," he said excitedly. "It's not far."

For the next half hour, they cleaned up the RV scrubbing the milk from the floor, putting away the blueberry pie and putting away the tea cups. Ingrid made a lunch from sandwich fixings from her cooler. They put on bathing suits just in case it stayed warm enough to swim.

Derek gathered the gear from the compartment under the Flair-two life vests, two paddles, two folding chairs and a red Coleman bag for the sandwiches, soda, fruit, cookies and water. At the last minute, Ingrid threw in two towels and two sweatshirts. From time to time, they would stop and hug remembering last night and needing to reconnect to the warmth of last night. Then, they would busy themselves with their impending excursion.

"Are you sure this boat isn't going to sink?" she questioned as she stepped in. She pretended to hesitate with one foot in the boat and the other on land.

"Com'on you're a Norwegian, of Viking descent. Norwegians don't sink," he said feigning a captain's position holding the lead rope by the end of the canoe as she got in.

Once on their way, they paddled in even strong strokes. Now on the clear steady waters of Sebago Lake, it seemed there was no possibility of sadness, just serenity. The sun warmed his back as he followed her fluid movements. Blond hair glistening in the sunlight. Her shoulders rose and fell with every stroke. He remembered every detail of last night in the sight of her rhythmic movements.

Ingrid wore a white light weight shirt over her black bikini. The outline was visible beneath. The white shirt was in stark relief to her tanned skin. She covered the places where he kissed her last night. This morning, watching her move, dipping the paddle into the clear water, in rhythm with hers, took on a whole new meaning. Again, he was surprised by his feelings. It was as if he had re-entered a place he once knew.

Can't believe I feel this way he thought. So involved, so soon. Maybe it's just because she lost her husband and me, Jenny. I don't know. But I love being with her, looking at her, touching her. This has to be some kind of reaction to being alone so long but it feels real. Really real!

The water was dark blue with ever green pines on the shoreline providing contrast to the soothing waters. Fluffy white clouds that looked like marshmallows punctuated the lighter blue sky. A perfect day.

"Delicious!" she said.

"What's delicious?

"This day," she responded and he knew exactly what she meant.

They canoed around the perimeter of the lake avoiding the occasional speedboat that interrupted their peace. At noontime, they found "their own private island." It had a small cove-like area with rocks encircling a sandy beach. The waves broke over the rocks and lapped against the shoreline. Since it was on the backside of the island, it was out of sight of the world.

After Ingrid got out, Derek dragged the red canoe up between two rocks tying the rope to a tree branch. She set out their towels - two chairs, two sandwiches, two sodas, and two people - their own private place.

"Delicious," she said not to him but to herself.

"Easy," he returned. They laughed and kissed automatically. As she looked up at the sky, Ingrid knew that this moment, this day would stay with her forever. No matter what happened tomorrow; this was their "forever moment." The sound of the water lapping against the sandy beach, the sight of the loons passing by dipping out of sight from time to time, and his kisses. This was their moment.

When she turned to look back at him, she looked deeply into his eyes, trying to see if he sensed the importance of this moment. For the first time, she noticed the horrific sadness that had been so apparent earlier was gone. It had been lifted for this moment. His eyes smiled back at her for an unprotected fleeting second.   Then, almost as if in embarrassment, he looked toward the sky.

After lunch, feeling the sun burn into his skin, Derek pulled her to her feet, picked her up and deposited her into the lake. She screamed and splashed him in retaliation. Just as he was about to dunk her again, he remembered the square bandage showing through her wet shirt.

"Oh, I forgot! Your bandage! The water? Is it OK?

She waved him off with her hand, "It's OK - no restrictions. I took a shower, remember," she reassured him. Relieved he splashed her back a little more carefully and ran for the shore. Ingrid dove in and swam out a few yards. He noticed her rhythmic strokes and immediately knew that she had perfected the art of swimming. Again, he experienced her natural beauty.

Then quickly returning to the beach pointing to the bandaged spot, she said, "Don't want to push it." Instinctively, he leaned over, lifted her shirt and checked out the bandage and finally kissed her right above the sore spot. As she lay down to dry in the sun, she realized she felt better whenever he did that even though she didn't know why.

My God, she thought, we have only been together a few days and it seems forever. We're like teenagers and a long time married couple all together. I just enjoy him so much. I love this kind of innocence and spontaneity. His dark hair and handsome face match him so well. He's like the first boyfriend I never had but always wished I had. This has never happened to me before. It can't be happening so fast but it is!

Lying beside her with his arm around her waist, he wondered why he felt so moved by her, so in need of protecting her. Might it be the loss of Jenny and Zack, a post-traumatic stress thing, or had he finally begun to put aside some of his self-absorption to fully appreciate someone else's plight. Jenny had always been kind of protective of him. This was very different. Her words interrupted his thoughts.

"You know, at first I was very upset about the biopsy, and I'm still worried, but it had a good side too," she ventured.

"Good?" he questioned not understanding.

"Well, after Svein died," she explained, "I was so stuck in myself. So afraid to give myself physically to a man. Maybe afraid of more hurt, more loss, I don't know."

She shifted to face him, "Last night, I realized that I could give myself to you as a whole woman-before anything more happened to my body. Not that I expect it to…"

He listened.

"The biopsy helped me to appreciate myself, my health, my sexuality, as it stands right at this moment. I feel like I was jolted out of myself." He thought about what she said and realized she found "the good side of a bad situation." Derek appreciated her attitude, her honesty and openness. Jenny died with a great deal left unsaid. It was never her way. This was new to him and he liked it.

After a few minutes of comfortable silence, he added, "This morning I realized when I came here I was devastated over the recession, Lehman Brothers, Morgan Stanley, my future, my career. Money, money, money!" He went on, "I felt as if I couldn't be visited by any more bad things happening. Then, I realized if I hadn't felt pushed to the brink, I might not have retreated to Sebago Lake. And found you. That's the good side for me. You!"

Suddenly Ingrid blurted out, "I knew we would make love last night. I just knew." He laughed at her abrupt change in tone,

"I didn't know but I hoped, " he teased drawing her closer.

"You hoped?" she teased pushing him away. Again, he held her tighter. For a long time they held each other kissing from time to time, snuggling beside the red canoe.

In time, the breeze began to cool as the smooth waters began to look like a coarse uneven fabric. Derek knew this lake and knew they should heed the wind and weather. So, they packed quickly, and urgently paddled back hugging the shoreline. There at Sunshine Camp, they gratefully returned the canoe.

Later that night, they went to dinner at the Sebago Resort Club. It was a wonderful prime rib dinner in a quiet dining room, with candles and roses on the table. The only thing that was not so wonderful was the inevitable knowing that Derek would have to go back to work tomorrow. He knew he had no choice.

"It was like a veiled threat," he told her over coffee. "This morning my boss said that he understood my need to get away and clear my head but that I was needed there. He pointedly told me that in this crisis there would be some decisions made-about downsizing to save the company."

"I understand," she said reaching out for his hand.

"The implication was that if I couldn't be there to be a part of the solution, he might consider me part of the problem. You know the language," he added holding firmly onto her hand. Now, the language of their hands was more telling than any words.

"I put him off as long as I could. He wanted me there today. I said sometime after noon tomorrow," he grimaced at the thought of leaving.

"At least we have tonight and tomorrow morning," she answered.

As soon as she said it the words fell flat. She thought we haven't had enough time. Can't even think about him leaving tomorrow. Can't imagine going back to how I felt before. To being alone-to the worry about the biopsy without his protectiveness. Maybe he's overly protective because he lost Jenny and Zack but I don't care. Don't care. It feels good to be cared for like this. Now that this has happened how do I go back? God, I don't want him to leave!

It was early when they got back to the park. Derek retreated to the RV for a few minutes to check his Blackberry for messages as Ingrid ventured over to the shower to wash her hair. They decided to build a "last night" fire to use up the wood they had accumulated.

A cool September night, the lantern was lit, the recliners were pulled up to close to the fire, and camping blankets were hung over the chairs to ward off the inevitable chill.

"I can pack up the RV in the morning. Besides the fire is a good excuse to cook some "s'mores." Can't go camping without them," he concluded putting a marshmallow on a stick.

"Glad you thought of it, " she said breaking the graham cracker squares in half, placing pieces of dark chocolate on top of them getting everything ready for the blazing marshmallows.

They ate as many as they could but finally gave up knowing they couldn't finish the whole package.

"I'm done!"

"Me, too!"

The fire was blazing persistently tumbling over itself with red and orange light, huge pieces of charred wood were visible beneath the flames. Their lounge chairs were pulled close to each other until she realized she could fit in the largest one with him. So, she moved over. He welcomed the move so for a long time they stayed huddled by the fire, covered by the warm blankets not wanting the night to end.

"I'm glad I found you."

"And me, you, " he answered.

Derek stoked the fire but quickly returned to her adding, "I can't believe I came here to get away and be alone and you came here to get away and be alone. And this happened. It's almost like some powerful forces moving us along-like in a movie or novel. Just the right moment. Just the right place and time."

"I know," she moved in closer as she adjusted the blanket.

"It was like everything was going bad. The final straw was my job. Then, that all changed when I found you here," he whispered as he leaned over to kiss her.

"I feel it too. The comfort, the ease, the end of emptiness for me. And I don't want it to end," she said softly.

"I don't want it to either!" he said quickly reassuring her. "It doesn't have to! Do you doubt it?"

"No, No! Not at all but we do have other important things in our lives to consider," she said thinking of their work, her health and her daughter.

"What could be more important than this?" he asked directly.

"Nothing, you're right." Somehow at that moment she knew that they would find a way to be together, no matter what happened to them separately. This was no time to waste the present moment by being afraid of the future.

"We'll find a way to be together, OK?" he reassured her.

"Yes, I believe you," she whispered.

Then, she returned his kiss as the fire raged on. He held her close and she pulled him even closer to her. They kissed again rekindling the passion of the night before.

"Let's go in."

"OK."

Once again, painfully aware of the inevitable separation that was soon to come and dreading the morning light, they slept with each other not beside each other that last night at Sebago. That night they came together with a passion that had been smoldering all day. It was like this might be their only moment; the rest of the world did not exist. The past was gone; the future was not in sight. Just the urgency of each other's physical needs.

They made love to the rhythm of the gentle sound of the waves caressing the shore. This night they were free to enjoy the warm softness of each other's touch coupled with the urgency of the impending loss of that touch coming so soon the next morning. The fire in the grate outside at first had burned briskly but as the evening wore on, it settled into a smoldering dim light. Finally, it burned itself out into dark embers as a golden harvest moon stood guard of the darkness waiting for the inevitable morning light.

Chapter Twelve

The next morning the sun was bright, high in the sky; the beach had barely visible grey footprints freshly made in the sand. Imprints from sandals and bare feet alike blended together.

Two loons came into view swimming side by side. One would disappear for a time only to appear again. Surfacing and resurfacing the loons reemerged-two black heads rising high in the water - wings stretching and shaking off the clean, clear water. Again, the wistful cry.

Two solitary figures were huddled there on the beach as the straight, sturdy pines green against the blue sky guarded this time, their parting moment. Alone by the lake, they kissed goodbye.

"Are you sure you won't come with me? I'm worried about leaving you alone in that tent," Derek interjected looking back at the campsite which was too neat, too clean to be welcoming.

"I'll be fine. You found me here when I was alone," she said trying to reassure him.

"But that was then and this is now.'"

"Wasn't that a book title?" she quipped to ease the tension. She put her head on his chest trying not to cry.

Frustrated to have to end this he blurted out, "I know this is crazy, but I loved being with you! I love everything about you!" he said in a voice that was low and full of passion. "I love you."

"And I love you. Now, go or I'll cry. We'll talk soon," she said turning her head away but still holding onto him, still trying not to cry.

"I'll call you tonight," he said pulling away making his way to the RV. Without looking back, he moved quickly into the driver's seat stopping only for one final look at her there on the beach. When he left, she began to cry.

That night when Derek called she plugged her cell phone into the charger in her car so she could talk longer. They hung on savoring every moment. Not wanting to end the conversation until they knew exactly when they would see each other again, they decided to meet in Worcester, Mass at the 99 Restaurant the day after next. He would get out a little early and meet her as she passed through on her way home to Connecticut. Then, satisfied they would soon see each other again, they were able to say goodnight.

The next day the weather turned cold as a front from Canada enveloped the campgrounds. Ingrid retreated to her tent where she wrote in her journal. Then, on the following day, her last day, Ingrid packed her tent in the trunk, neatly arranging it so it would fit.

Finally, she walked over to the beach and then back to #148 where he had been. She stood silently for a while. The ranger drove by in his golf cart as he wondered what she was doing. Her white wool cap was pulled down over her golden hair. Her bright red sweater was a reminder to him that before long it would be Christmas.

"Are you alright?" he asked

"Yes, oh yes! Heading out today."

"Have a safe trip."

The leaves on the trees were beginning to fall now. Most of the camp was shut down to campers as everyone prepared for the long, cold, Maine winter. She drove by the signs along the exit road saying "Closed For The Season."

"That was me. Before I came here. I was half alive. Closed For The Season," she said aloud. On the ride home, she fondly remembered every moment of their September days at Sebago. Excitedly, she drove down the Maine Turnpike, to Route 495 and finally on to Worcester.

She had set her GPS to East Central Street Worcester, Mass. As she turned onto Route 209, her heart began to beat more quickly. Pleased to be meeting Derek so soon, she glanced at Holy Cross College, high on the hill to her left, and then followed the GPS directions off the exit onto the crowded grey streets of Worcester. Once in the parking lot, she spotted his Mazda. Quickly checking outside, she found him in the cozy booth in the back of the 99.

They both smiled broadly and hugged fondly as the other diners watched. Everyone in the room sensed the joy in this meeting.

"It's wonderful to see you," he said.

"And you." She stole a quick kiss across the table. Then, she moved into his side of the leather booth to be nearer. The obvious delight to be together again was reassuring to them because in some ways their meeting at Sebago seemed like a dream. Now they were out in the real world. The 99 meeting brought continuity-a transition from one world to another. After the waitress took their order, they caught up as he asked about Kari's adjustment into college, and she asked about being back at Morgan Stanley.

"For now, we are stable," he offered. "But there's talk of a further government bail-out and down-sizing the firm. Somehow, I'm not as frantic as I was. Being with you these last few days has helped." She nodded her head and smiled as if she understood. They lingered as long as they could making plans for further meetings. She promised she would call him as soon as she had news from Dr. Bacon.

"Speaking of the biopsy," he began. "I don't want to get ahead of this but my friend and client is Dr. Brunell, who happens to be an accomplished oncologist at Dana Farber Cancer Center. Craig and I were roommates at Cornell. If there is any question about the…" he added hesitantly but deliberately.

"Thanks for that. It's comforting to know but I'm hoping it will come back benign-like before on the other one," again she hesitated to bring this to him but he persisted.

"No, no, I mean it. I want you to have the best medical care possible and Dana Farber is known to be the best. You can stay with me in Hingham any time you need to. Just so you know…" he trailed off when he saw the fear in her eyes.

"I'm getting ahead of myself. It's just that I want you to know that I'm here for you."

"Thanks, sweetheart," she said hugging him not wanting to let go. The waitress hovered over the table picking up a plate here and a glass there.

Saying goodbye in the 99 parking lot was poignant and painful at the same time. They set a tentative date for his first trip to Connecticut. They would visit Kari at UConn on the same week-end. They kissed good bye as the rest of the world looked on.

Finally back on Route #290, Ingrid pushed the speaker on her phone and dialed Kari. "Hi, honey, you will never believe where I am. I didn't want to tell you this before but I met a wonderful man."

"What? When? Where?

The ride from Massachusetts to Connecticut was full of details as a mother tried to convince her daughter that it was alright for her to be with another man other than her father. Ingrid had purposely decided to wait to tell Kari because she knew she needed time to explain. Now with her phone plugged into a permanent charge, she could talk for a longer time and not lose the connection as she had at the campsite.

Kari was happy for her Mom but also felt a strong pang of loss. She had been her mother's protector for all these past months and now it seemed someone else was stepping in. In another way, she was relieved because she had to go on with her life too.

"I want to meet him for myself," the daughter concluded.

"Of course, as soon as we can. He wants to meet you too. We thought we would come to UConn for a game and meet you in the next couple of weeks."

"And I had another date with Ted. I like him, Mom, but it's not serious yet. I'll keep you posted.'

"You better," the protective mother said. "Maybe we'll meet him on that week-end. We'll talk tomorrow, OK. Love You." Before she knew it, Ingrid was passing the Connecticut Rest Area where she pulled over to get a soda. She knew she should get out and stretch because she still had to finish the last leg of the trip on RT 84 onto RT 2 to Glastonbury. Suddenly that late hour and emotional evening caught up with her and she couldn't wait to get home to her bed.

Since it was late when she pulled into 256 Georgetown Drive in Glastonbury, she decided to unpack the Cruiser in the morning. She knew that in a few days she would be immersed in her work at Loomis Chaffee. The start of a new school year was right around the corner and it would take her full attention. In the next few days there would be the meetings and usual preparation. During those days she held close the thought of seeing Derek again. His frequent calls to see "how she was doin" warmed her and kept their special memories alive.

On the first full day of school, Ingrid returned to Georgetown Drive tired but exhilarated. A typical first day of classes. Picking up her mail at the entrance of the condo development, she found a card from Derek. Excitedly, she opened it. "Thinking of You" was its major message. As she entered her front door, she was still smiling. the sharp ringing of the phone startled her.

"Yes, Dr. Bacon. Inconclusive. I see. Another Consult? Possibly another biopsy?" her voice sank and her smile quickly faded as she mentally resisted the idea of going on with the fear of breast cancer that she had been grappling with for months. Secretly, she doubted the competence of this local gynecologist, this local hospital.

Having this threat of breast cancer hanging over her life was a heavy burden for her. Now she was remembering the loss of her mother, just 59 years old, who died when Ingrid was barely in her twenties.

But again, she had known many women in the church who had survived cancer-and many who hadn't. These days fear seized her at times, often before she fell asleep. Other times she was captured by an appreciation of the moment and relished this time of "not knowing." However, now she did what she had done to get through the days after Svien's death. She turned to her faith and prayed silently.

"The results were inconclusive, you may need another biopsy. As soon as possible." For about an hour, she sat motionless in her living room looking absently out the picture window. As she held Derek's card in her hand, she examined and reexamined it as she looked intently at her favorite birch tree in the front yard. Finally, she called Kari and Derek.

Kari was frightened and disappointed by the doctor's words but reminded her mother not to project into the future but to just deal with today. The daughter repeated words her mother and father had spoken to her when she was troubled.

Derek's response was far more proactive. After their first week-end in Connecticut, he suggested she could meet him in Boston to do the biopsy, if there was to be another one, at the Dana Farber Center. A second opinion. "I know I can arrange for you to see Craig. He's the best. I'll call him in the morning and get you a date and time. I'll be able to go there with you. You shouldn't have to do this alone."

At first, Ingrid hesitated to bring this problem to Derek but then he convinced her that he would <u>not</u> have it any other way. He has proven to be protective by nature she thought. It reassured her. He would call her as soon as he knew the appointment time. She finally agreed. She slept restlessly that night but she slept.

Chapter Thirteen

The following Friday night Derek came to Ingrid's Glastonbury condo. When he pulled into the driveway, he checked to see that he was taking # 256, the correct parking spot. She waved to him from the picture window. As he bounded up the stairs at the side of the building, he felt his heart skip a beat.

She opened the door before he could ring the bell and nearly knocked him over with her fierce hug. It had seemed like several months instead of several days she thought. Once inside the living room, Derek noticed the pink rugs and the delicate, airy decorations of her place. A small statue of a Greek goddess was placed on a side table under the picture window. There were family pictures with a cozy paisley sofa and ivory colored shades on brass lamps.

"It's so much like you," he said as he made a sweeping motion with his hand. "Just like you."

Then he took her in his arms, moving away from the picture window and into the hallway between the dining room and the kitchen. She lead him up the back stairway to her bedroom.

"Wait! Are you alone?"

"Of course," she said laughing.

Their love making took away her fears for her health and his apprehension at meeting Kari the next day. He knew how important Kari's opinion of him was to her mother. But all those thoughts disappeared as he once again gently kissed the slightly healed pink scar on her breast. She felt reassured by his kiss and then inflamed with a longing that had been pushed beneath the surface of her reality for many days. Now she allowed that longing to come forth and meet his passion.

Afterwards, they stayed in bed, not wanting to leave the security of each other's arms, but needing to plan the next day's trip to UConn. Derek told her about his conversation with his friend, Dr. Craig Brunell. She listened intently as her mind was brought back to the cruel reality of her need for more testing. She planned her next trip to Hingham to meet with Dr. Brunell at Dana Farber.

Suddenly, he said, "Hey, we missed supper."

"I know the best pizza place. Are you game?" she said sitting straight up looking at the clock on the bedside table. "Get dressed. I think they're open til ten."

At supper that night, they continued to make plans as they consumed what Derek called the best pepperoni pizza he had ever eaten. Ingrid filled him in on all the latest news of Kari's dates with a new guy called "Ted". She didn't know his last name yet but Kari seemed excited about him. Anyway, they would meet them both tomorrow at the UConn football game.

The next morning was cold and grey as most fall days in New England seem to be but it was perfect football game weather. For Ingrid and Derek the grey day didn't deter them from enjoying a long leisurely breakfast. They talked of the first breakfast they had ever shared at Sebago. By noon, they were ready to make their way down Route 84 to Exit 69, a trip the mother had memorized by now. She had come to know the campus well in a short time.

"At the gate, we'll meet you under the West Side Sign," the mother reassured her daughter as she drove towards Storrs. As they drove through Mansfield, she noticed the traffic which was heavier than usual. When they reached the campus she pointed out the Co-op where she and Kari had lunch and across the street the gym where the famous UConn Girls Basketball Team played. They crawled along through the sprawling campus.

They finally found parking at the Stadium Parking Lot which seemed miles away. The crowds were huge and uncontrollable so it was difficult to meet anyone under any sign but they waited.

I hope she likes me he thought. Not used to thinking of a child who is really an adult. Never had to so I don't know how to act. Just relax he counseled himself knowing how nervous he was meeting someone so close to Ingrid.

Ingrid could sense Derek's nervousness so she reassured him, "Just look for a blond who looks and acts just like me. She will love you. Because I do." He smiled.

Finally, he saw the blond who looked exactly like the woman he loved and sure enough she met and hugged her mother. Then, she nervously introduced her new boyfriend, Ted, to her mother. She hugged Derek right away and said, You must be Derek." Introductions were over. Easy!

By the time they got into their seats Ingrid was catching up with Kari while Derek and Ted were yelling out the football plays. Both men were happy to let the diversion and excitement of the game take over the afternoon.

After the game, Derek told them that he would take them to The Outback Steak House if they could find their way there. He was sure he'd seen a sign on the way into Mansfield. Ted had been there with his parents the previous weekend so he knew the way. Once they were seated, Derek realized he knew Ted's mother and father from Quincy, Mass. He had done some business with them through Morgan Stanley. Ted began to relax as he realized Derek knew not only his parents but some other close family members. The two men were able to ease the tension for each other with this mutual connection.

"Ted and Laura Stevens. I never would have made the connection unless you mentioned that your father was with The Housing Authority in Quincy. We met at a fund raiser back in April. He mentioned that you were in the process of deciding on a college," Derek said. "He was with your aunt and uncle, Chet and Phyllis, I believe."

"They live on the same street as we do. It has always been a big family affair at Christmas and Thanksgiving. I'll be going home for the turkey feast in a few weeks," Ted offered. "My Dad and Uncle Chet own the local plumbing supply company-Stevens Plumbing, " he explained. "They're looking for me to major in business but I'm keeping my options open."

"It's early in the game," Derek answered.

Mother and daughter were able to connect face to face for the first time since Ingrid got the news from Dr. Bacon. Ingrid found it easier to explain her plans to visit Dana Farber on the following week-end with her daughter sitting across from her and with Derek sitting across from both of them.

"Dr. Craig Brunell is the leading man in Oncology at Dana Farber," Derek told Kari, "and he just happened to be my roommate at Cornell." Kari then turned her interest to Derek as she asked him about himself. She expressed her sympathy for the loss of his wife and child in that tragic crash but he turned the conversation back to his interest in her and her college studies and plans. Meanwhile Ingrid asked Ted about his choice of UConn and how it came about.

Kari really liked Derek and Ingrid liked Ted. The only difficult part of the evening was that it ended too soon, everything else about it had been perfect. On the ride home from Storrs to Glastonbury, Derek explained his association with Ted's family which gave added reassurance to the mother.

"A wonderful family. His Dad is kind of a self-made man. Known to be honest and hardworking. A family man. A close knit family that gives back to the community, " he said as he drove her little car down Route 84.

"And Kari is a delight to be with. Looks just like you. You must be so proud of her."

"I am. We've been through so much together. I'm lucky to have her. She seemed relieved when you explained your association with Dr. Brunell. What a perfect first meeting. And I'm delighted you knew Ted's family."

As they pulled into Glastonbury Center, they decided to stop at Dunkin Donuts where they revisited the day over a shared coffee roll and a cup of coffee. Neither one wanted the evening to end or the morning to come when Derek would have to drive back into Boston.

The next week dragged on as Ingrid learned the names of her new students. She corrected papers, made up a quiz for the substitute teacher she would have on the following Monday. On Friday, she prepared her students for the upcoming quiz and left detailed notes for her replacement for that day. Her principal was the only one who knew of her mission in Boston.

On Friday, she left early right before her last study hall. Driving to Boston, she felt a sense of urgency, apprehension over what Dr. Craig Brunell would advise. Of course, she worried about having to have a mastectomy or worse losing her life to this deadly disease. She started to pray. It was her only recourse. She had to go one step at a time and for tonight she would be with Derek. She knew they would make love again just as she knew it the first time they found each other. Her fear always was that she would lose him after having just found him. She worried that he might not find her attractive if she had surgery. It frightened her but for tonight she couldn't wait to be in his arms, to feel his hand on her breasts. She knew she would savor every kiss, every moment of their togetherness.

"You're so good to be here for me now," she whispered as they snuggled by the fire. Her blond hair glowing in the firelight, her face uplifted to his.

"There's something I need to tell you," he began. "After losing Jenny and Zack, I went through a difficult process. At first, I was bitter and angry, mad at the world, unable to cope with any sadness and hurt. Then, I met you and you brought me back to life. Literally, you gave me a reason to go on."

She arched her shoulders, raising herself up on her hands, turning her face towards the fire thinking he would say he could not endure any more loss, any more pain. Pain like she herself had felt with Sevin's sudden death. Derek saw the fear in her face and put his hands on her forearms turning her towards him.

"No, wait! I need to let you know this. They are gone-never to come back again. But you are here. Do you understand? You are here! It doesn't matter what happens in the future, to your body. You're here with me now. I can never hug Jenny or Zack again but I can hug you. I can talk to you; I can see your face. You're alive and here right now! That's all that matters to me."

Ingrid felt the tears falling on her shirt. She didn't even try to wipe them away.

" But I didn't want to bring all this to you," she said softly.

"You are bringing me You! And you're perfect just the way you are," he whispered as his arms encircled her holding her as tight as he dared to.

Ingrid knew that some moments take on a life of their own. This was such a moment. One that would become burned into her mind forever. The words Derek whispered that night became the mantra she used to pull her through the visit with Dr. Brunell the next Monday. When he told her he would conduct another biopsy to review it before making his decision, she remembered that moment. When he said that if there were any question in the findings, the best approach might be a thoroughly aggressive one-to do a lumpectomy. Now, it seemed Ingrid would travel to Hingham almost every week-end.

One week day, on her way to work, Ingrid met Carla at the Dunkin Donuts on Main Street in Glastonbury. This was their way of seeing each other face to face since Ingrid was gone on Sundays and unable to go to Asylum Hill Church services with her. They hugged enthusiastically as the other morning coffee drinkers looked on. Carla cut right to the chase by asking, "How's your "new guy" with this latest health predicament?"

"At first, I was scared he would turn away. Can you imagine we just met and this happens?" Ingrid said as she motioned towards her body and carefully sipped the hot coffee.

"But?"

"But it's not like that. There was this one moment on the first night I stayed in Hingham when he explained 'I am here now' he said, 'My wife and child are gone. I can't hug them or talk to them.'" Ingrid whispered in the same passionate tone Derek had used. Carla pulled in closer and nodded her head to show she completely understood. Ingrid continued to explain.

"He's made me understand that he learned from his loss to appreciate what he has <u>not</u> lost, to appreciate what he <u>has</u> now."

Carla took a moment to think as she sipped the coffee that seemed to remain undrinkable and hot forever. "You're so right. It could have gone the other way, he could have been afraid of sickness and more loss. That's why I asked."

Ingrid smiled to herself. "But he hasn't. We're closer than ever. If Dr. Brunelle decides to remove the tumor, I can't imagine being with anyone else. Right now, I'm just taking it one day at a time - and praying for a good result."

"I'm praying too." Carla added as she reached over to hug her dear friend. Then, remembering the work day ahead of them, they quickly finished their morning coffee break and scurried off to battle Route 91 and the Hartford morning traffic.

After the second biopsy, Dr. Brunelle did suggest that she have a lumpectomy to remove the tissue just to be sure. He could test more thoroughly at that time. Derek was with her when the surgery was done at Dana Farber. This important day proved to be the beginning of a long period of months that would include many trips to Dana Farber, a series of radiation treatments that Dr. Brunell suggested instead of a radical mastectomy. The fall of 2008, beginning with this initial surgery, was a blur of stressful procedures to help ward off the cancer.

That day a dark haired nurse entered the recovery room when Ingrid was waking up from the anesthesia. Derek was sitting beside her bed holding her hand. A warm blanket was placed on her body as a nurse's aide checked the monitor beeping behind her blond head. Derek followed the attendant's every motion, while waiting patiently for Ingrid to stir.

At first she moved ever so slightly in the bed, moving her hand in the direction of her chest. He gently steered her hand away.

"Sweetheart," he whispered leaning into the bed.

She opened her eyes, just slightly, trying to decide if she might open them fully.

"It's over. You're doing fine, " he reassured her. She smiled vaguely.

When she was fully awake, Craig Brunelle appeared at the end of the bed. As always Derek was happy to see the familiar face of his good friend but now even more the professional face of her doctor. He reached for his hand waiting to hear his words.

"It went well. I'm confident that I got it all. Of course, we will do further testing. But, I'm confident." He smiled reassuringly at Ingrid.

"When will she know," Derek asked.

A groggy Ingrid interjected, "How long?"

"In about ten days we will get together again after we make sure there are no more surprises here." The doctor smiled again as Ingrid weakly smiled back.

Seeing the fearful weariness in her eyes, Craig then spoke directly to Ingrid, "It looked contained. Like a simple tumor. This should be conclusive. My nurse will call you when we can visit and wrap this up. Good job."

When, like most doctors on their rounds, he quickly began his exit, Derek walked him out knowing his friend would be completely honest with him.

In the hall he said," I see a lot of these and you did the right thing getting here early. Don't worry, we'll check it out." Then, "I see she's very special to you and that means she's very special to me."

"Very special, " Derek agreed.

With that, Craig playfully punched Derek's arm and walked off to the next patient. Ingrid was unable to hear their conversation as she lingered in that place between sleep and awareness. Then the nurse came in, carrying a small white cup with two white pills.

"For nausea," she said handing them to Ingrid. She gently raised her in the bed to help her swallow the pills.

Ingrid could feel the pain of the bandage reminding her of the wound. At first, it troubled her wondering how scarred she would be but then she realized how glad she was to have the tumor gone. She settled back to rest as Derek returned to continue holding her hand. They spoke intermittently as the anesthesia wore off. He reassured her that Craig was positive, very much acclaimed for his work, and would give her case special attention. She believed him.

Later that night, Ingrid was fully awake and able to leave the hospital to return to Hingham. Once again, Derek reassured her that he was happy to be with her, happy that it was over, and grateful that his friend, Craig, had the knowledge and skill to help. Both of them realized he was a good man to have in charge.

For a couple of days she stayed in the big old colonial home that had been cleverly decorated by Jenny and still carried her memory. Kari drove up to be with her on the second day and noticed how attentive and kind Derek was with her mother. By Sunday, except for a little soreness, Ingrid was feeling much better. So, Kari drove her mother back to Glastonbury.

On the ride home, Kari asked, "Do you think you might marry Derek, Mom?"

"We've been so pre-occupied with my health. There's been no time to think about..."

"But what do you think? Maybe?" The concerned daughter went on.

"Don't know yet but I think we're very lucky to have found each other, after having so much loss," the mother cautiously added not really knowing where the conversation was going or how Kari felt about her mother committing to anyone other than her father.

There was a long pause in the conversation as Kari stopped to get a ticket entering the Mass Pike. Once they cleared the toll booth Kari added, "Just so you know, I think he's great." For a moment Kari's thought drifted back to a mental picture she held of her father in the pulpit delivering his sermon. For a moment she felt like she was betraying him or his memory. She wasn't sure which.

Then she thought of the past two days and how attentive and kind Derek had been to her mother. She liked him. She felt compelled to add, "Even though Dad can never be replaced."

"I know. I understand there can never be anyone like your Dad, but Derek is special too," Ingrid conceded in a small weary voice.

As they pulled into Georgetown Drive, Kari helped her Mom out of the car. When Ingrid winced a little, pushing herself up to get out of the seat, her daughter took her arm guiding her up to the back stairs and up to the front door. Still holding her up, she maneuvered the key with her other hand to unlock the door.

Once inside, she helped her mother up to her room and made sure she went right to bed. "Rest now, we'll talk later," Kari said as she moved quietly down the hall to her room which seemed warm and comforting especially now that she was spending so much time in a dorm room. The last thing she saw as she drifted off to sleep was her favorite picture of her Mom and Dad.

In about ten days Craig Brunell did report inconclusive findings and outlined an aggressive three months of chemo and radiation therapy for Ingrid. Just to be safe. She agreed.

The early fall months went by as Derek stood by Ingrid reassuring her, telling her to trust Craig and the care at Dana Farber. In the early weeks she went to school, corrected her papers and went to Hingham on week-ends. Then, she was able to take eight weeks sick time to stay in Hingham and complete the course of treatment. Miraculously, there were no early winter storms that year making it possible to practically commute from Connecticut to Boston.

Sometimes when Ingrid was very tired, Derek stepped in and drove her to her appointments. He sometimes told his boss he needed extra time off or to work from home. Even though Morgan Stanley was taking over Bear Stearns and the work load had doubled, Derek kept up by staying at work later, when he wasn't with Ingrid; therefore, when he needed time off he got it. When she lost her hair from the chemo, he bought her a colorful hat to wear as they walked in Boston Commons. When she felt better, they would have lunch at The Lennox before walking in the park. Derek had a way of making things OK even when they weren't.

Chapter Fourteen

inally, in late January 2009, Dr. Brunell told Ingrid she was free to go, and enjoy her life. Of course, she would return for checkups but for now she was done. That night they sat by the fire in Derek's old Victorian parlor and drank wine, celebrating life and their love. It had been five months since Sebago but both agreed it seemed like five years. Now they would be free to meet on weekends without a medical schedule.

Ingrid returned to Glastonbury looking forward to going away to Okemo in Vermont the very next week-end. They would ski and sit by the fire each night. But a nor'easter came in making the roads impassable so they were snow-bound-with one hundred miles between them.

"I can't believe this," Derek said putting down the phone and feeling cheated by the weather. Then he realized that they were still free. For now, her health was cleared by Craig. She was fine.

This was only one week-end. She had a winter vacation coming up in February. He thought of St. Martin and the wonderful clear water, the white sand beaches. There was a time when he would never consider going to a place where he had been with Jenny but not now.

The next week-end, he approached the subject.

"I have an idea," he said excitedly. "Do you have an updated passport?'

"Sure but..."

"Let's go to St. Martin."

"When?"

"February vacation. I have enough frequent flyer miles for both of us."

"Are you serious?" she said as a broad smile presented itself. She leaned in closer to him. "Of course, you're serious. That's one of the things that attracted me to you in the first place. Your love of 'surprises'. It would be so perfect after the last few months. And I've never been to the Caribbean. Do you think we can?"

"We can't _not_ do this. I'll work it out at work next week. There's some vacation time simply because I never took one. You'll be off and we can go," now his broad smile presented itself as he imagined the warm sun and the lazy days of St. Martin.

They arrived at Princess Julianne Airport on February 21st. Excited to have time with each other, they looked forward to ten days of warm weather, and stress-free moments to love each other. On the plane Derek fell asleep as Ingrid read David's Baldacci's *One Summer*, a novel she picked up at the terminal in Boston. He slept while she cried when Jack was dying in the early chapters, and at the end of the book was silently cheering for Jack when he rallied to save his daughter, Mikki, from drowning. This was her relaxation, her "fun" reading, her diversion from the classics. And his deep sleep was his complete collapse from the everyday tension of Morgan Stanley, the rising and falling stock market and the fears of the future of the American economy.

Derek woke up just as the pilot asked the stewardess to "prepare for landing." He whispered, "I guess I was more tired than I knew." Again her broad smile.

" It's been hectic for you, sweetheart. Take it when you can. I read most of my book. A few tears," she said as she fanned her hand in front of her face to hide her emotion. He leaned over and kissed her forehead.

"My sweet Ingrid," he whispered appreciating her sensitivity. They held hands as the stewardess walked by them checking the space in front of them and the angle of their seats. She put her hand on Derek's head rest to signal that he should bring the seat forward for landing. He did. They landed in one smooth motion and again the relaxed broad smiles reemerged.

They picked up their baggage on the carousel and looked for the Hertz Car rental sign. After checking at the information booth, they took a van to the Hertz lot in Simpson Bay just beyond the airport. As they boarded the van, the warm air encircled them and a gentle cool breeze swept away the heat.

Feeling the warm breeze, Ingrid sat back and enjoyed this moment. She didn't mind that her very short hair had a golden pixie look. Her first trip to another country with the man she loved. When the attendant began to speak French, she answered him in his language. Her early training shifted into gear. Derek stepped back-proud and impressed. Then, when they arrived at Porto Cupocoy, a new development in the Dutch Netherlands, she spoke to the desk clerk in Dutch. Again Derek was admiring the cosmopolitan side of Ingrid.

In the elevator, she modestly explained, " I can function in a limited way in many languages but I wouldn't want to go beyond that." None the less, he was impressed.

On their first night, they decided not to explore the island but walk down the hill to The Gourmet Marche, a local supermarket of sorts. Since it was on the Dutch side, the clerk readily accepted American dollars. Here they picked up a baguette of freshly baked bread, water, sliced salami, gouda cheese and wine.

That night in their room, they enjoyed the delight of the simple feast they prepared, and the delight of being free from cancer, and being together. They took long luxurious showers in a spa-like white tiled bath, and made love in a wonderful soft bed covered with a thick white down-filled comforter. A warm breeze drifted in to envelope them. They curled up in this space until they drifted off to sleep. The magic of the islands touched the pink scars on her breast and began to speed up their healing. The magic of the islands allowed Derek to savor her presence beside him and diminished the deep pain of aloneness that had chased him nearly every night since Jenny and Zack died. Both knew they wanted to hold onto this peaceful warm, white comfort at Port Cupocoy, Saint Martin forever.

The next day, they decided to find a beach on the French side of Saint Martin. At breakfast, an English speaking local told them that the most romantic beach was on Pinel Island. "Just go to Cul de Sac, just past Phillipsburg, and follow the signs. Oh, and take the shuttle to the island," he added. Trusting they would find their way, they ventured out navigating the narrow streets. Soon they saw signs for the French Quarter and Pointe Blanche, and finally Cul de Sac and Pinel Island.

"We have to take a shuttle boat," Derek reminded himself out loud. Then, Ingrid noticed a group of tourists gathering at the dock ahead. They joined the group in line and were quickly taken to a lovely beach nearby. By moving quickly, they managed to snag a couple of comfy chaise lounges at the very end of the beach away from the other beachgoers. It was perfect-a bit removed from all others and a couple of feet from the warm Caribbean waters.

All afternoon, they drank in the warmth of the sun, talked about their lives at home, their lives together. There was something magical about this sensual place-the white sand and the warm water. Being here seemed like a dream come true. It reminded them of being on Sebago Lake where they met and fell in love; yet, it was more sumptuous, more surreal, more filled with edges of beauty. Everywhere they looked was the crisp blue sky meeting the blue green waters with the occasional white-sailed boat dotting the horizon. And it was their togetherness folding into this place, the comfort of loving each other. At times, even though it was overwhelming, they simply held hands and it was enough.

They ordered lunch and drinks which were brought to their table. They resisted the heat of the day by huddling under the umbrella and swimming often and long. They held onto each other in the water but no one seemed to notice. Some of the women bathers were topless but it seemed natural. Ingrid protected her scars from the direct sun with a sheer over blouse and covered her short hair with a lacy sun hat-that was far more sexy than the topless ladies of the island. Even her short blond hair was distinct and notable because it never darkened, even when wet. Derek loved the way she looked on this day.

Later in the day, the dark skies started to threaten as a few drops drove most tourists back on the shuttle boat. Not wanting this precious day to end, they stayed on until 5PM, the last shuttle.

"One last swim," she said. Derek watched her walk into the water. Her multicolored bikini was molded firmly to her perfectly proportioned body. Her newly grown shorter blond hair glistened in the sun. Just before she dove in, she turned and gave him a little smile. Clearly, even on this beach for nude swimmers, she was the most beautiful woman. She didn't need to uncover her body with its recent scars to be seductive. She had a natural beauty.

Something happened to Derek at that moment. He knew he wanted to ask her to marry him, to set a date. They had talked of marriage, with both being in favor of marriage, but neither knew just "when". A plan was formulating in his mind. Before this vacation was over, it would be settled.

The sun warmed his feet and legs as he stretched out on the chaise lounge when a shadow from the coarse beige umbrella cut across his body. He watched her swim, her smooth mesmerizing strokes. Then a stray cloud cast a shadow on the soft blue water. For a brief moment, he thought of Jenny and Zack-a sense of betrayal.

Here I go again! Reaching back to those old feelings. No, I won't do this. Blame them for my not going on. It's not fair to them. Jenny would want me to be happy. I would want her to go on if I left her early. A scene flashed through his mind as he remembered a grief counselor session when the therapist said, "You are not your wife, you are not your son. What are <u>you</u> going to do with <u>your</u> life?" The dark cloud past by just as Ingrid emerged from the water to take her place beside him. He knew what he wanted to do with his life.

The next day, they visited Phillipsburg. It was Valentine's Day. Finding a place to park on the narrow streets of the capitol city was almost impossible. Colorful shops lined the sides of the streets. Hawkers and venders set up shop wherever they could. People from the cruise ships milled around. The center of the city was closed to traffic so the streets were mobbed with pedestrians hopping and weaving in and out of each other's way. Here were the incredible store fronts with diamonds and gold jewelry-each window filled with tempting watches, diamond rings and bracelets.

"The Dutch are known for their diamonds," she shared, "the Swiss for their watches."

Derek had a plan when he said, "Let's just look." She was unaware. Not knowing what to expect but curious to see the jewelry, she went along. He had looked at diamond rings in the jewelry building on Washington Street in Boston where he bought Jenny's ring. So, he had an idea of what he was looking at and could compare prices, and quality.

They wandered into Oro Diamond on Front Street but found their jewelry more commercial. More for the tourists Derek thought to himself. Ingrid followed along, letting him take the lead.

"Some of my clients invest in diamonds," he told her. "I'm interested in the value here on the island." She heard him but kept trying to steer him to the incredible men's watches-the Carl F. Bucherer and Frank Muller models from Geneva. He maneuvered her to a case of rings in Shiva's. They were simply stunning. Some took her breath away.

"Try this one on," he said eagerly. The clerk picked up on his eagerness as Ingrid pointed to the ones she liked best. When she tried on one in the center case, she didn't have to say anything. He saw the way she looked at it on her hand and he knew. It was a 2 carat square diamond with an ornate setting of many small diamonds. A small price tag with 3,500 dollars written on it was hanging on its side. As Ingrid walked to the small oval mirror where she could see how the ring looked on her hand, Derek asked pointed questions about origin, weight, cut and clarity. He knew this ring was well priced. After a few minutes, Ingrid reluctantly took it off and moved to the front of the store to a case of men's watches.

Not wanting to lose a sale, the clerk said to Derek, "We have a policy. You do not need to give us payment until you go home with it and have it appraised." Gesturing to the clerk, Derek let him know that he would consider and be back soon. Within an hour Derek had slipped away from Ingrid and returned to Shiva's to buy that ring. His mind was made up now and all he needed was the perfect moment-and for her to say "yes". Confident and excited, he was certain about his decision.

They stopped at Pandora in Phillipsburg to pick up a couple of beads for Kari. One was a silver turtle and the other a colorful pink and purple round disk. Derek sat on a wooden bench outside the shop waiting patiently as Ingrid looked over every bead feeling the need to pick out the right one, exactly the right one. They walked on down the crowded street until she saw a small beaded purse that would be perfect for Carla. When they got to the duty free perfume shop, she found some Gucci Flora for herself.

"I'm happy with my shopping," she said. "It's perfect." Still she didn't suspect.

"I have a surprise," he divulged with a boyish grin on his face.

"What now?"

"I made a reservation in Grand Case at L'Auberge Gourmande for tonite. Best French restaurant on the island. We got the last two seats. Valentine's Day I guess."

"I'll trust you on this one." She said as she took his hand. They decided to go for a swim in the pool at the Porto Cupuocoy before taking the ride over to Grand Case. On the slow moving narrow road, they passed the harbor side in Marigot, the capitol of the French West Indies, where they saw colorful booths set up in long rows. The bright reds, oranges, cobalt blues, lilac in the native vendors booths drew them in.

"Bon Jour, Madame, hats, shirts? Can we help you?"

They were nearly assaulted by offers as they maneuvered through the narrow aisle between the booths. Again she held his hand. Each booth seemed identical with beads, dresses, bags, T Shirts, men's hats and all kinds of handmade trinkets. Many had St. Martin written on them. Derek seemed nervous constantly checking his pocket to see that the ring was still there.

Then, he carefully withdrew to the center of the confusion to sit on a stone bench. When Ingrid was done buying a few postcards and a colorful bowl, they made their way to L'Auberge on the main street in Grand Case. Even though Derek had been there with Jenny on his last visit to the island, he was anxious to share its sunny elegance with Ingrid. They found a parking space on a narrow side street and made their way past the Tastevin, another Grand Case restaurant known for its French cuisine, to the bright yellow columns of the L'Auberge.

Once there, they anxiously stepped past the porch where diners were already seated. Inside, they were seated in a quiet corner at the back. Derek thought this the perfect place for him to propose. Soft yellow walls were decorated with giant delicate floral paintings, while the dark, ornate wood beams on the ceiling offset the airiness of the all yellow interior. A perfect, private romantic setting he thought. White table cloths, fine wine goblets, and heavy silverware provided a touch of elegance.

Being drawn in by the old world elegance, Ingrid whispered, "This is lovely."

"I knew it would be perfect for Valentine's Day," he added as he took her hand. The waitress interrupted when she offered complimentary champagne. When they both nodded in approval she poured the golden fluid into fluted glasses. Since the menu was in French, Ingrid assisted Derek who finally settled on "Beef Filet in moral mushroom sauce" and she ordered "A rack of lamb with fois gras."

Their meals were served on hand painted china plates with a floral design. For desert they settled on white and dark chocolate and crème which they ate in small spoonful's from one plate. The presentation of their meal was nearly as delicious as the food itself. Ingrid realized that this night, this place, was the most special Valentine's Day she had ever experienced. As the champagne settled in, she realized how grateful she was to be healthy, to be here with Derek at this moment. She thought to herself that life could not get more beautiful than this one moment.

"Do you know how much I love you?" he asked suddenly.

She looked up smiling, "And I love you too. Happy Valentine's Day, sweetheart. I have never been happier." Then, he knew it was the right moment.

"I want to be together-just like now. Every Valentine's Day. For as many as we can." She nearly interrupted him telling him that, of course, they would be together but she remained quiet, sensing this was different for him.

Suddenly, he got up, went to her, kneeled down and leaned over to her. He whispered, "Will you marry me?"

The reality of the moment struck her when she saw the ring in his hand. The same beautiful diamond she had tried on that day. At first, she was too stunned to answer but she had already decided that when <u>he</u> knew, she would also <u>know</u>. There was no question. Just like the beginnings at Sebago Lake, they both always knew pretty much at the same time.

"Yes, yes I will marry you," she whispered into his shoulder as she hugged him. He put the ring on her hand and bent down to kiss her. Then, he kissed her hand as if to seal the engagement. She smiled at the gesture.

The other diners, lost in their own enjoyment of this magical place, at first seemed not to be paying attention but suddenly a couple in the corner began to clap timidly. The rest of the room followed suite with a dignified but appreciative celebration of the moment. Finally, when they left, several couples offered their congratulations, others nodded and smiled. This was their happy moment and others seemed to want to be a part of it.

For the remainder of their vacation on St. Martin, Ingrid and Derek continued their happy celebration as they explored the island. From time to time Ingrid would look down at her hand surprised to see the diamond there. When Derek saw it, he was proud and sure of his decision.

One day they ventured over to Bard de'Embrouchere where they learned to windsurf. That night when they had supper at The Galion Hotel on Orient Beach, they met ex-patriots, Pat Turner and his wife, who ran the restaurant there. They were quick to congratulate them and offer champagne for their engagement.

Another day, they returned to Phillipsburg to eat crabs at the Air Lekkerbek Bar and Restaurant. Derek shared that this was Zack's favorite experience on the island. Eating in the hull of an airplane. Another night at the Antoine restaurant, Derek remembered his last night there with Jenny. She was very sun burned and not too comfortable. Ingrid understood that all these memories were a part of what she loved about Derek. She understood his need to share, thanking him for being willing to bring her to St. Martin.

On their last day, they followed the road down to the French Cul de Sac to Anse Marcel. Once there, they made the steep climb to Pic Paradis. "Paradise Peak. We had to do this," he said as he looked out over the island. Now as he saw her, with sweat on her brow, standing there at the top beside him, he realized that they had made St. Martin their own. No longer did it belong to him, to his past, but to them. He looked forward to coming back to St. Martin when they were married,

Chapter Fifteen

The following September, Ingrid and Derek were married on the shore at Sebago Lake. After the ceremony they returned to the Sebago Lake Resort for a small reception with friends and family. People would say, "Why Sebago Lake?" But somehow the question never got answered. Ingrid would look at Derek and smile, "Why not Sebago Lake?" Ultimately, there were no more questions.

They made their vows, just past the camping area, on the far right side of the beach facing the small island. Reverend Jaslow, a local Lutheran minister, whom Ingrid had known from years ago, performed the simple ceremony. Derek choose his parents to stand with him while Kari and Ted were Ingrid's witnesses.

In the past year, Ingrid had grown to love and appreciate Ted who'd proven to be a steady, loving boyfriend for her daughter. She already considered him as part of the family. He and Kari were talking "marriage after graduation" or perhaps during their junior year. The mother approved.

Earlier, over spring vacation, Derek and Ingrid had flown to Asheville, South Carolina so his parents could meet Ingrid. They saw their son's happiness and eagerly gave their approval of her and the pending marriage. As an only child, Derek knew he needed his parents to stand with him for this special ceremony. Somehow, he knew it would alleviate some of their previous sorrow, softening their worry over their son, and offering a new beginning. It did.

After the ceremony Ingrid and Derek lingered a few minutes on the beach. They clung to each other promising to return in September each year.

"No better place to renew our love," he said holding her tightly.

"I can make that promise," she whispered. This was their special promise, their private marriage vow.

As they pulled away from each other, the sun broke out from behind the clouds and set the water afire with light. Each little spire of gold danced on the water's surface. It warmed them. The crows cawed and the loons cried again.

At the Sebago Lake Resort the main dining room was quietly elegant with large arrangements of callillys, dainty Saint Anne's Lace, and white roses offset with candlelight. The bride and groom joined Reverend Jaslow and his wife, Ruth, Derek's parents, Carla with her new fiancé, Kari and Ted with his parents and their friends from UConn, and a number of colleagues from Loomis Chafee and Morgan and Stanley. A small gathering of about thirty people.

The Resort was "off season" so most guests stayed the night enjoying the local band, "Wayne form Maine" who played long into the night. The next day after a buffet breakfast out by the water, the happy couple left for their honeymoon destination-a week in Norway.

Although no one ever really answered the question, "Why Sebago?", most guests felt they found the answer in the simple beauty of the way the sun rose over the lake that morning. The natural beauty of the morning was predictable. It fell into place with the simplicity of Ingrid and Derek's love; its glory put aside past sorrow and welcomed in a new time blessed with a more natural order of events.

Over the next ten years, this pattern of natural predictability held true. Kari and Ted did marry at the beginning of their Junior year. By the time they were ready to graduate their first born, a boy, named Svein after his grandfather, had arrived. Two years later, a girl, named Ingrid after her grandmother, was part of the family. Ingrid remained healthy and cancer free to enjoy her grandchildren. Their life took on a simple predictable pattern of holiday dinners, babysitting Svein and little Ingrid, and South Carolina visits to Derek's aging parents during February school vacation.

Since the recession in 2008, Derek held steady in his job struggling to help the company come back after the initial bail-out and the prolonged economic downturn. Then in 2012, he moved over to a position at JPMorgan. Knowing that unemployment was high, he hung on at that bank job even though he didn't agree with some of their practices-to pay off his house in Hingham and support himself and Ingrid.

In 2010, several months after their marriage, and after her resignation at Loomis Chafee in 2009, Ingrid was accepted for a part time position at Andover Prep in Andover, Mass where she taught Greek and Roman Literature. In 2012, she signed a contract for a full time teaching spot. Knowing that Derek's job was precarious, they both saved diligently.

Predictably, every September Ingrid and Derek returned for a visit to Sebago Lake. It was their time to get out the camper, pull up to their favorite site and sort out their future. When in 2013, the FEC fined JPMorgan 1.3 billion dollars with a criminal probe ensuing, Derek began to worry about his own financial security and their future. Then when Jamie Diamond stepped down as Chairman and CEO, he knew he had to prepare for early retirement.

By the campfire they decided to retire to Maine as soon as they could. In 2018, Derek was offered an early retirement so he took it. Predictably, they took their savings and bought a quaint cottage in South Casco Bay just five miles from where they met. They researched the market and finally were able rewrite the Hingham mortgage, to pay cash for the cottage through Fannie May. It was a bank owned, foreclosed property which needed a lot of "TLC". So the ad said. For several years, they poured their tender love and care into this lake side retreat bringing it back to life. A new roof, a new furnace, and a new kitchen.

Now, every summer the grandkids could come to Sebago Lake where Ingrid could teach them how to swim and Derek could show them how to fish. Predictably, the locals had begun to call Derek, "Holland", last name only and Ingrid, "Blondie". They began to settle into life on the lake preparing for the time of Ingrid's retirement in 2020 when they would sell the house in Hingham and live here full time.

For a couple, whose early life had been marred by unpredictable tragedy, these ten years of quiet predictability were welcome. Like a drink of cold water offered a marathon runner, they drank up the ordinariness of their existence never failing to appreciate each moment. Each day, each child, each morning of health and happiness. Their love did not fade but grew more and more intense. It was a tangible force that anyone could see, more extraordinary than the predictable and ordinary life they lived. Their connection to Sebago Lake became a symbiotic, symbolic one that constantly renewed that love.

In the summer of 2020, the first full year of Ingrid's early retirement from teaching, Kari, Ted, little Svein, and little Ingrid spent the last two weeks of August at the cottage. The house in Hingham went under contract in early July. This year Ingrid and Derek would stay on full time at Casco Bay. Their simple life would only be interrupted sporadically by trips to South Carolina for relief from the winter's cold.

Now in the last days of August, the long parade of boxes was over except for the last few things in Hingham which were to be retrieved after the closing on August 30th. At night, Ingrid dreamed of packing and unpacking boxes. She dreamed of the relief she would feel when settled in one place. Then, of course, she would remember the unopened boxes that filled the back storeroom of the small cottage. The ones that have her notes and books on Classical Literature and Writing. She just couldn't throw them away without going through them.

Also included in the treasures in the back storeroom were two boxes of mementos from her early life with Svien and Derek's remembrances of Jenny and Zack. Ingrid kept Svein's diploma from Seminary, some of his sermons, and a few early pictures. Derek kept many pictures of Jenny and Zack, their marriage certificate, Zack's birth certificate and their death certificates. How could he throw these things out? These painful, powerful, poignant things, that they could never part with but couldn't look at every day, were carefully tucked into brown cardboard boxes in the back room. These extraordinary remnants of earlier lives remained contained and safe while they continued on with their ordinary everyday life.

The whole family swam off the dock; they fished; they cooked lobsters in a big blue pot. They ripped open the claws with the red "pincher things" that the kids loved to use. They pulled the husks from the native corn and boiled it. They slept with the windows open. Predictably, they watched the sunset every night. August in Maine at Sebago Lake.

During this vacation, Kari, who was usually pre-occupied with her own motherly duties, chasing a ten-year-old boy and answering the questions of her eight-year-old girl, noticed that her mother seemed unusually tired.

"Have you lost weight?" she started.

"About the same, I think," her mother said avoiding the question. She continued to scrub the lobster pot and wipe the counter in the kitchen.

"You seem more tired than usual..." Kari offered but Ingrid kept tidying up the cabin. She and Derek would go back to Massachusetts before Labor Day to close on the house in Hingham and to pack the last few boxes.

"We will be finished with the house on August 30th. It's been hectic with leaving Andover, selling the house and everything. Just everything together, I think." She made a circular encompassing gesture with her arms to show the depth of her frustration as she finished her chores.

Kari dropped the question but vowed to make Derek promise he'd arrange for a check-up for her with Dr. Brunelle at Dana Farber. Before she left for home, he had promised her! The mother noticed the daughter's concern and expected her to enlist Derek's help. She didn't mind.

I know I'm emotionally exhausted she thought. Just so tired of so many changes. Will be strange to see the school buses bringing the kids to school. Will miss the kids. Kind of who I am-the teacher-my identity. Love the kids! No more bells, no more schedule. That part is great! So this is the right time to end it. Just tired of so much transition with moving and retirement together. It will be better after Labor Day.

Later after all the family good-byes, when they settled into the silent of "no grandkids around." Derek asked her about getting a check-up with Craig.

"I will see Craig at the end of September," she promised, " after we have had our special time here." He understood. Reluctantly, he agreed knowing not to push her but that she was true to her word.

On August 30th Ingrid and Derek drove to Massachusetts one last time to sign the closing papers for the

Hingham house. Earlier in the day they put the last few boxes into the truck and watched silently while the agent and the new owners made their final "walk through" inspection.

Driving home they were silent for some time until she spoke.

"Are you satisfied with the sale?" she asked him gently knowing this was the first house he and Jenny and Zack shared together.

"The time was right," he answered. She could see a trace of the old pain in his face. "You know when it's the right time to do something. In these past weeks, every time I saw something around the house that I wanted to hang onto, I was able to reach inside myself to that "knowing" that this was the right time to move on."

" So you're OK with it?" she whispered.

"Yes, and I'm grateful you were able to let me have all this time there with the memories," he said reaching for her hand.

"Of course, those memories are a part of you and I love all of you," she gently traced a pattern of soft touches on the back of his hand as they finished the trip in silence.

It was late in the afternoon when they arrived back at Casco Bay. The dust from the gravel road charged up ahead of the heavy Tacoma Truck that Derek loved so much. Ingrid lingered in the front seat moving slower than usual. This fatigue was not lost to him yet he was determined not to mention it-to make this year's September visit a memorable one. One to commemorate their life together. Silently, he opened the heavy car door as she lightly pushed it forward. Again silently, they gathered their belongings; Ingrid's favorite Norwegian sweater that she bought on their honeymoon, his fishing gear stacked neatly in the bed of the truck.

"You go in. I'll finish this." He motioned her towards the front door. She was glad to stop moving and just be in one place, so she went in. As he pulled out the fishing rods with their angular lines attached to them, he felt a pang of relief as well as a familiar quick sharp pain in his chest. It disappeared in a second just as it always did. It had been with him ever since he lost Zack and Jenny. Then he thought about how fishing had been his passion, his only escape from the constant pressure of the financial crises that were his life for years. Now he would fish every day.

Once inside they moved about the kitchen in an unspoken ritualistic dance. She took the food from the bags, one by one placing it in its proper place; he opened the blinds to reveal the singular view of the lake and then gathered the firewood. Taking the kindling from its place, he lit their fire. A strange peace came over them. They were home.

This easy way stayed with them as she prepared the food and he set the table. Then watching her by the sink, a lingering worry. She just didn't seem right. He looked at her more closely. She noticed but just smiled at him. His mind flashed back to the times she was recuperating from the cancer. But this was different-a pervasive fatigue. Maybe, she's anemic he thought.

And then the terrible thought maybe the cancer is back again. His chest tightened again. Instinctively, he knew he had paid a price for the recession in 08, for Jenny and Zack's tragic deaths, for the uncertain economic times these last few years. When he felt the heaviness in his chest and the quick pain, he was reminded of all the pain he had felt. Then, he would breath in deeply, relax and remind himself that he had to set up the chairs on the deck before dark.

The exhausted couple retreated outside to their beach where two bright blue Adirondack chairs waited. He carried a bottle of their favorite local wine; she brought cookies and small cupcakes.

Ribbons of darker blue touched the light blue sky as the water filled the bay. The waters were calm; the pale white and grey formation of tender clouds hung over head. The caws of seagulls were the only sound near the shore. Then, off in the distance a lone motor boat made its way along the shoreline. The sun was dipping in the sky making a cone like shape on the water. They sat quietly and listened.

The sound of the motor boat diminished, the seagulls stopped squawking, and a lone loon sent out its sharp cry. Suddenly, four black heads surfaced only to be quickly lost again. The repeated cry of the loons greeted the dying day. Surfacing and resurfacing the loon family reemerged black heads rising high in the water, wings stretching and shaking off clear, clean water. Again, the cry.

"Remember our first year here, over at the State Park. It seems so long ago but not so long," he mused.

"Can't believe we took a chance on each other. Seemed like it was other forces at work. Like it was meant to be," she added.

"Looking back," he offered "it seemed so right." Then, he laughed, "because it turned out so right, I guess."

"Pretty scary-me-alone-in a park-in a tent. Now I can't imagine it," she said.

"I'm so glad I found you, sweetie," he answered taking her hand turning towards her and noticing her color as ashen in the dim light. Then, he felt the need to reiterate the point to make sure she understood.

"Really glad because I love you so much now."

"Even though I took you on a roller coaster ride of chemo and radiation that first year." Images of his steady presence by her side during treatment at Dana Farber came to mind. But there were also images of walking in the Boston Common while her hair slowly grew back. She brought up these memories and spoke of her gratitude and her love for him.

"You know I always worried that it might be too much for you but you never flinched," she squeezed his hand and leaned over to kiss him. "Even when we decided that I should give up my lease, move into the big house, resign from Loomis. Even when you were struggling at Morgan and Stanley, you were there for me. For us."

"No, no, no! You were the one who was there. Right from the beginning. I was so glad you were alive and with me. Even recuperating and getting better every day."

Then his voice softened, "I could never imagine losing you," he kissed her hand and looked directly at her.

Then, playfully to break the mood she said, "What about when you made sure to lose me? In St Martin. When you sneaked away to get my ring." She looked down at the diamond that even now sparkled in the late summer sun. A happy memory enveloped them as they watched the sun getting lower in the sky. They listened for the next cry of the loon.

"Did you know that the loons will soon fly to salt water, the adult loons leaving their children there to make their own way. Next year, they will come back here without their offspring to raise another family," he informed her.

"Just like we do, I guess," she observed. "As I look back, I realize that Kari never would have given herself permission to go on, to marry, to have her children so young, start her own life-if I hadn't gone on with mine. We were too dependent on each other after Svein died."

"So, I did have a purpose," he joked.

"Oh, yah - great purpose," she teased in her exaggerated Norwegian accent. Then, she went to his chair to sit beside him. When they bought these Adirondacks at Aubuchon's, she picked the large double size, just for this purpose. Large blue and white striped pillows covered the backs and seats for comfort. A hammock hung from the tree nearby. Some late blooming Queen Anne's Lace were hiding there in the long grasses.

They hugged and hung onto each other as the sun began to set. Silently, they watched it slip below the horizon. The green, grey water reached out to the darkened beige sand slapping the wooden deck pilings. Their small motor boat moored there rocked back and forth in a brisk breeze. And once again, the plaintive sound of the loon punctuated their quiet space.

During the following week, Ingrid and Derek relived their original September at Sebago. One sunny, crisp day they took a picnic out to the cove on the island: the cove they had claimed as their own so many years ago. Then, of course, they went to Naples for a ride on a seaplane. This time they searched for their own cottage nestled into the shoreline in Casco Bay. They even spent a day at the Fryeburg Fair watching the Horse Pulling Contest and eating lobster rolls.

At the fair Derek noticed that Ingrid seemed weak but determined to push herself to relive each precious moment of their early days together. Then on the morning of the 30th of September, just before they left to make the trip to Boston to see Dr. Brunelle, she asked to go to Sebago Lake Park for one last quick visit.

They pulled into the dark, damp abandoned park and made their way to the beach. The morning sun was breaking in bursts of welcome light. Then, it came fully front and center like a revelation that hides in the recesses of your mind until one day you understand some great thing. The sun broke out into its full glory. Its warmth spread over them as they sat on a log sipping coffee and eating sweet coffee rolls from the Dunkin Donuts.

That morning Ingrid had taken her bright red jacket from the back bed room and found herself a scarf to match. The beginning of a new season she thought. She knew she was anxious about the tests that morning. Afraid really. She knew she had been weak lately. But still she wanted to look her best.

When Derek looked across at his wife, she was wiping away a small tear from her cheeks. Yet, not wanting to worry him, she quickly smiled at him.

"It will always be beautiful here," she said hearing a singular cry of a loon.

"Not nearly as beautiful as you are at this moment," he answered hugging her close to him. This was a moment she knew she would never forget. A moment that held some special tenderness. They sat in silence while he wondered what will I ever do if I lose her? What if it happens again? He held her tighter.

***

Several seasons later, as always, the loons returned to Sebago Lake. Now a new family, all were traveling in a row up above the water line, now diving below. Their lonely cries rang out piercing the silence.

Late in the afternoon, a lone woman sat on the beach. Seeing the line of loons ducking and disappearing, she remembered when her husband told her that story about the loons. Now it seemed as if their cries were mocking her.

How ironic that he should go first she thought. He worried about me because I was the one with cancer. Even when he made sure I had a check-up, he didn't get his. How ironic.

In her sixties, Ingrid felt old now even though she still had a natural beauty about her. Two men, too early heart attacks. My God, how could I ever have seen that coming she thought.

In this moment, she really missed him. Sighing, she breathed in this place, with the warm September sun making her face flushed. She watched the clouds separate and come together making different distinct patterns up above. Sometimes, they seemed to overlap and bump into each other: some white, some a musky grey. Still the same clear water, the same green pines, the gentle lapping of the waves against the shore, and the soft beige sand under her feet. Everything the same but so different!

How can all these things be the same when everything is different? That question haunted her. Now she wondered about the wisdom of her coming here today. Kari and Ted begged her not to but she felt impelled to come to this spot. His spirit was here. She knew it. She looked over to site # 148 and #149 remembering their first few days together. She pictured the roaring fire, the Fryeburg Fair, the ride on the Ferris wheel and the gentle kiss on her forehead. Then, flying overhead in the Seaplane and making love in the Flair that night.

The September sun warmed her bare feet. She looked out at the dark green waters. A breeze shifted direction leaving a touch of cooling air where it had been. Later memories came flooding in as she remembered the walks in the Boston Commons, St Martin. She watched as the diamond on her finger picked up shafts of colored light. The later years with their gradual return to Sebago Lake.

Oh, how she missed him.

Then all the earlier memories blended into one. The thought went through her that she was grateful for their time together. And it all started here. In one unpredictable chance meeting. She realized she wouldn't change one moment of their time together for any other minute in time. And that it didn't have to happen at all but it did-by chance. It was a perfect life together, a perfect love. Now she wiped the tears from her face.

The sun began to sink into the horizon. Slowly. Silently. The cry of the loon cut sharply into the silence. She shivered as the air grew colder with heavy clouds gathering over darkened waters. Reluctantly, but resolutely, she left when the sun was completely gone from the sky.

www.ingramcontent.com/pod-product-compliance
Lightning Source LLC
Chambersburg PA
CBHW060418310726
48976CB00003B/1099